Barbara Cartland, the world's most famous romantic novelist, who is also an historian, playwright, lecturer, political speaker and television personality, has now written over 350 books and sold over 370 million books over the world.

She has also had many historical works published and has written four autobiographies as well as the biographies of her mother and that of her brother, Ronald Cartland, who was the first Member of Parliament to be killed in the last war. This book has a preface by Sir Winston Churchill and has just been republished with an introduction by Sir Arthur Bryant.

Love at the Helm, a novel written with the help and inspiration of the late Earl Mountbatten of Burma, Uncle of His Royal Highness Prince Philip, is being sold for the Mountbatten Memorial Trust.

Miss Cartland in 1978 sang an Album of Love Songs with the Royal Philharmonic Orchestra.

In 1976 by writing twenty-one books, she broke the world record and has continued for the following six years with 24, 20, 23, 24, 24 and 25. In *The Guinness Book of Records* she is listed as the world's top-selling author.

In private life Barbara Cartland, who is a Dame of Grace of the Order of St. John of Jerusalem, Chairman of the St. John Council in Hertfordshire and Deputy President of the St. John Ambulance Brigade, has fought for better conditions and salaries for Midwives and Nurses.

She has championed the cause for old people, had the law altered regarding gypsies and founded the first Romany Gypsy camp in the world.

Barbara Cartland is deeply interested in Vitamin therapy and is President of the National Association for Health.

Her designs "Decorating with Love" are being sold all over the U.S.A and the National Home Fashions League made her, in 1981, "Woman of Achievement".

Barbara Cartland's Romances (Book of Cartoons) has been published in Great Britain.

By the same author in Pan Books

The Dangerous Dandy
The Ruthless Rake
The Bored Bridegroom
The Penniless Peer
The Cruel Count
The Castle of Fear
A Very Naughty Angel
Call of the Heart
The Frightened Bride
The Flame of Love
Say Yes, Samantha
As Eagles Fly
An Arrow of Love
A Gamble with Hearts
A Kiss for the King
A Frame of Dreams
Moon Over Eden
Fragrant Flower
The Golden Illusion
No Time for Love
The Husband Hunters
The Slaves of Love
The Ghost Who Fell in Love
Passions in the Sand
An Angel in Hell
The Incredible Honeymoon
The Dream and the Glory
Conquered by Love
Love Locked In
The Magic of Love
The Taming of Lady Lorinda
The Wild Cry of Love
Kiss the Moonlight
The Marquis Who Hated Women
A Rhapsody of Love
Look, Listen and Love
The Wild, Unwilling Wife
The Curse of the Clan
Gypsy Magic
Fire in the Blood
The Island of Love

The Outrageous Lady
The Passion and the Flower
Love, Lords and Lady-birds
The Hell-cat and the King
The Sign of Love
The Castle Made for Love
A Fugitive from Love
A Runaway Star
A Princess in Distress
Flowers for the God of Love
Lovers in Paradise
The Drums of Love
The Prince and the Pekingese
A Serpent of Satan
Imperial Splendour
Light of the Moon
The Duchess Disappeared
Terror in the Sun
Women Have Hearts
A Gentleman in Love
The Power and the Prince
Free from Fear
A Song of Love
Little White Doves of Love
Lost Laughter
Punished with Love
The Prude and the Prodigal
The Goddess and the Gaiety Girl
The Horizons of Love
The Waltz of Hearts
Dreams Do Come True
A Night of Gaiety
The River of Love
Gift of the Gods
Love at the Helm
An Innocent in Russia
Love Wins
The Wings of Ecstasy
Tempted to Love
Love on the Wind

For other titles by Barbara Cartland please see page 156.

BARBARA CARTLAND

WHITE LILAC

Pan Original
Pan Books London and Sydney

First published 1984 by Pan Books Ltd.
Cavaye Place, London SW10 9PG
© Cartland Promotions 1984
ISBN 0 330 28285 9
Photoset by Parker Typesetting Service, Leicester
Printed in Great Britain by
Hunt Barnard Printing, Aylesbury, Bucks

68435090

01859936

Author's Note

The demand for coal began to increase rapidly towards the end of the 18th Century. After James Watt had, in 1781, made his improved steam engine capable of driving other machines, industry needed power.

The development of the Railways demanded not only coal for themselves but supplied Industrialists all over the country. The expansion of coal was dramatic – 10 million tons in 1800, became 12 million in 1870, and 95 million in 1913.

Other minerals rose in the same startling manner. In 1840 Britain produced three-quarters of the world's output of copper, half the world's lead and 60 per cent of its tin.

The Queen and Prince Albert's first journey by rail on 13th June 1842 gave Royal Approval to the "Age of Steam". In 1859 the Prince Consort opened the Cornwall Railway.

The Royal Railway Carriage was very superior, being oblong, measuring about thirteen feet by seven feet, and constructed of the finest mahogany. Double panelled, it was stuffed with felt to lessen vibration and increase warmth. The interior was lined throughout with delicate blue satin wadded and tufted, and the hangings over the windows were elegant draperies of blue and white tasselled satin.

Chapter One
1846

"The fog's gettin' worse, Your Grace!"

The groom spoke apprehensively, but the Duke made no reply, having obviously noticed it himself.

He had been forced to drive more slowly every mile and he thought now it would be wise to find somewhere to stay the night rather than press on to the Marquess of Buxworth's house where he was expected.

If there was one thing the Duke really disliked it was having his plans altered at the last moment, and if he had his own way he would have driven on, fog or no fog, until he had reached his destination.

It was this sort of determination which had made him the most outstanding athlete of his year.

First at Harrow where he had run a mile in four minutes thirty-six seconds, then at Oxford where he had excelled as an oarsman, while since he had been grown up he had won one athletic record after another.

He had climbed the Matterhorn, he had represented England in all the Fencing competitions in Europe and had been the winner every time, his horses had carried off the majority of the Classic Races, while in amateur Steeple Chases and Point to Points he was invariably past the winning-post ahead of every other competitor.

Apart from all this he was noted as a surpassing game-shot, whether of elephants and tigers, or of pheasants and partridges, so that his friends had long ago given up competing with him.

He saw that his vast estates in various parts of the country were run as smoothly as a well-oiled machine, which was due to the organisation and direction coming from the top, which was of course himself.

He often thought that there were few challenges left to him, but his life was so full and busy that he had no time to think about his past achievements, but had to concentrate on a day to day programme which would have exhausted most men.

At the same time he never achieved anything at the expense of his horses or any other animals that he was using for his own pleasure.

He thought now that, though he had no wish to stay the night in some uncomfortable Posting Inn, his horses should not be forced to travel any further in what he knew the groom beside him was thinking of as a 'pea-souper'.

Aloud he said:

"If I am not mistaken, Hanson, there is an Inn of some sort not far from here."

It was a long time since he had been on this particular road, but like everything else about him, his memory was phenomenal.

When a few minutes later they saw the flicker of distant lights coming hazily through the fog, he knew he had not been mistaken.

The Inn was rather better equipped than the Duke had anticipated, and since visitors who stayed the night were an exception he was able to engage the best bedroom for himself and insist that he also paid for the rooms on either side of it to remain empty.

In the past, especially in Posting Inns, it had annoyed him when the occupants next door had either coughed all night or else stumbled into the furniture because they had had too much to drink.

The Proprietor looked slightly surprised at such a request, but was only too delighted to rent the rooms to the gentleman who was obviously 'warm in the pocket'.

When the Duke also asked for a Private Parlour, it was made available.

Having ensured that his groom was also catered for besides his outstanding team of horses, he settled down to order what he required for dinner.

It was unfortunate that the brake which had been following was apparently lost in the fog.

There was just a chance that it would turn up later and find him, but he would not have been prepared to bet on it.

Because the brake was being drawn by six horses and driven by his Head Groom who was an extremely cautious man, the Duke was certain they would have stopped long before now.

They were doubtless in a larger and better-class Inn than the one in which he was now obliged to stay.

There was however nothing he could do but accept that he would not as usual have his own fine linen sheets with which his valet could make up his bed.

Nor would there be the special mats for his feet beside the bed and the washing-stand.

There was another groom travelling in the brake who was a better cook than Hanson who was accompanying him.

However Hanson could always be relied upon in an emergency, and the Duke, looking at the menu which the Landlord had produced, chose what he thought might be edible if Hanson supervised the cooking of it.

"I'll do the best I can for you, Your Grace," Hanson said, after he had stabled the horses, "but I'm not pretending I'm as good as young Henry. He be a natural, as one might say, in th' kitchen, for all that I'd trust him with any horse your Grace owns.'

The Duke looked up from the menu to say sharply:

"Sir! Remember, I have registered as Sir Ervan Trecarron!"

"Yes, o' course, Your – Sir!"

When the Duke was travelling he invariably used one of his lesser titles finding otherwise that people were so overcome at entertaining the celebrated Duke of Marazion that it became embarrassing.

He would also sometimes find himself the target of those who wished to get something out of him.

It was far easier therefore to be anonymous, and it was actually what he preferred.

"I'll get to the kitchen now, Sir Ervan," Hanson said, "an' I've taken your trunk upstairs."

He paused to ask anxiously:

"Ye're quite certain yer can manage by yerself, Sir?"

The Duke smiled.

"Quite certain, thank you Hanson!"

He was thinking as he spoke how on his travels in the Far East and in Africa he had managed perfectly well without the assistance of a valet, or anyone else except an illiterate, often half-witted native.

In fact, in the wilds he preferred to look after himself, finding that English servants required far too much attention and invariably grumbled at anything that was new and unusual.

Now he rose to his full height of six foot two inches and stood for a moment in front of the log fire which was blazing in the open fireplace, before he walked up the creaking oak stairs to his bedroom on the First Floor.

It was quite a large room, and as Hanson had already ordered a fire which was burning in the grate, the cold and damp outside did not penetrate into the low-ceilinged oak-beamed room.

The Duke's sharp eyes took in the fact that the room was surprisingly clean.

He was glad that unlike in many other Posting Inns he need not be afraid that the sheets on the bed would be dirty, or the blankets verminous.

Hanson with the help of the Proprietor had brought up a trunk which had been strapped to the back of his Phaeton just in case he was separated from the brake and the rest of his luggage.

Now he could see that it had been opened for him so that he could take out what he required.

Because he had been driving for many hours the Duke took off his smart but slightly dusty clothes and washed in the warm water that had been placed in a can on the washing-stand.

He would have liked a bath, but he was quite certain it would cause so much commotion in the Inn that in consequence his dinner would be much delayed, as would that of any other traveller staying there.

He had no idea if there were other guests in the Inn because he had walked straight into his Private Parlour on his arrival, and not left it until he came upstairs.

Having washed thoroughly, thinking as he did so that everything might have been very much worse than it actually was, he took his evening-clothes out of the trunk.

He then dressed himself competently and far more quickly than if he had been assisted by his valet.

Actually, although he knew it would cause deep resentment if he said so, he preferred to look after himself.

Before he inherited the title, he had spent many months at a time in outlandish places where even the most elementary comforts were hard to come by.

Being alone constituted one of the challenges he enjoyed.

Yet he thought tonight the fog which had prevented him from reaching the Marquess of Buxworth was not so much a challenge as an obstacle and nuisance he had not anticipated.

He was quite certain that the Marquess, who had written an effusive letter of invitation to stay with him, would have arranged a dinner-party in his honour, and would be extremely disappointed at his non-appearance.

There was, however, nothing he could do about that, so the Duke dismissed it from his mind and taking from his trunk a book which he had been reading before he left home, he walked down the stairs and back to the Parlour.

He found, as he expected, that the claret he had ordered before he went upstairs was standing on the hearth in front of the fire and should, he thought, by now be at exactly the right temperature.

He poured himself out a glass which he found quite palatable and settled himself in an armchair to await dinner.

He opened his book at about halfway through the volume where he had left a marker, but found himself thinking of the purpose of his journey.

Would it really prove as fruitful as Captain Daltry had tried to make him believe?

Daltry had certainly been optimistically, wildly, enthusiastic about the whole project and the Duke found himself being almost carried away by the older man's persuasion.

'It is the chance of a lifetime, it is really!' Daltry had said. "I brought the offer first to your Grace for the simple reason that I know of no one to whom I would rather do a good turn, having been one of your whole-hearted admirers for many years!"

It was the sort of compliment the Duke was used to hearing, and he merely smiled faintly and waited for Captain Daltry to get down to what he thought of to himself as 'brass tacks'.

What it came to was that Daltry was selling on behalf of a friend a Coal Mine.

As he pointed out to the Duke not once but a dozen times, a Coal Mine was obviously something which every great Landowner should possess in the future.

Railways were being planned all over the country and coal would therefore be more in demand than it had ever been in the past.

As Captain Daltry pointed out, so many of the Duke's contemporaries already had Coal Mines under their land, and would undoubtedly reap the benefit of a demand that was increasing not only year by year but almost month by month.

12

Steamships had already revolutionised the means of transport by sea, and now, Captain Daltry said, with the coming of the trains, horses would soon become completly out-of-date.

"Not where I am concerned," the Duke exclaimed.

He had already travelled on a train and thought it was uncomfortable, noisy and dirty, but he was intelligent enough to realise it would undoubtedly become the regular means of conveyance in the future.

At the same time, the more he thought of trains the more he wanted to cling to his horses.

Almost as a gesture of defiance he was increasing the size of his stables and the number of horses he kept on the main roads over which he frequently travelled.

But despite all that, he was interested in what Daltry had to tell him although he did not particularly care for the man himself.

He had of course taken the precaution of finding out more about him, even though they had been introduced in one of his Clubs by a member whom the Duke had known for many years.

He had learnt that Daltry had served in India and had left his Regiment and that country without any suspicion of stigma against him, although it was hard to find anybody at home who knew him well.

"Daltry! Daltry!" men said reflectively when the Duke asked about him. "Yes, of course, I have met him on a number of occasions, on the Race-Course, at the Club. Seems pleasant enough, but I don't know much about the fellow!"

They all said more or less the same thing, but it did not tell the Duke what he wanted to know.

At least there had been no hints that Daltry was not completely open and 'above board', and certainly the papers he had left him to read about the Coal Mine were businesslike and gained the approval of the Duke's Secretary.

Because he never bought a 'pig in a poke', the Duke was determined to see the Coal Mine for himself and to gain some first-hand information about it before he put down his money.

"Surely there is no need to do that, Your Grace?" Captain Daltry asked. "As you see, I have brought you the report of several experts in that particular field, and I myself have visited the Mine on three separate occasions and been extremely impressed by its possibilities for the future."

"I agree with you. It certainly sounds excellent in every way," the Duke answered. "At the same time, I would rather enjoy a visit to Lincolnshire and have several friends in the neighbourhood with whom I might stay."

He had the feeling, although he could not be sure, that Captain Daltry thought it a waste of time, but if he did he was far too tactful to say so.

"I will of course be only too willing to show Your Grace the Mine, and anything else you wish to see," he said. "The surrounding country is pleasant, and the houses and villages you would also acquire in the deal are in reasonable repair. You might have to spend some money on them, but not much."

The Duke had looked up some of his friends who lived in that part of the country, and amongst them, with whom he intended to stay the first night, was the Marquess of Buxworth.

He was a lot older than the Duke and had been a close friend of his father's.

When he wrote to the Marquess asking if he could stay with him, the Marquess had written back saying nothing would give him greater pleasure than to welcome the son of his old friend.

The Duke then arranged that he should have a bed on the way home with Lord D'Arcy Armitage who was a member of several of his Clubs and also was a fierce competitor on the Race-Course.

With him, the conversation regarding horses, if nothing else, would be extremely interesting and he would certainly enjoy himself.

He had made no mention of the reason for his visit to either of his chosen hosts.

Captain Daltry had already warned him that he was getting in, as he put it 'on the ground floor', before anybody else knew the Mine was up for sale.

"It belonged to an old country Squire who had recently died," he explained. "His son has no idea of its potential value, and is obviously not interested in the countryside, prefering to spend his time in London."

Captain Daltry paused before he added:

"That is why Your Grace will be able to buy the Mine far below its true value. You will have to spend only a little money on new machinery and will undoubtedly have to employ more people than are engaged there at the moment. But that is something which should be kept at all costs from becoming public knowledge."

It flashed through the Duke's mind that he disliked subterfuge of any sort and preferred a straight-forward deal rather than to take advantage of somebody who was foolish enough to be ignorant of the Mine's true value.

As if Captain Daltry knew what he was feeling he said:

"Young Newall is an extremely foolish young man who has already dissipated most of the money his father left him, and if Your Grace does not buy the land and the Mine, it will doubtless go to some unpleasant speculator who will exploit the people working in it and extract every lump of coal greedily and without safety precautions, at the expense of those who work for him."

This was something the Duke knew had been exposed in a report published in 1842 which had shocked and horrified the British Public.

Since then safety in the Mines had been much improved but there were still unscrupulous Landlords who were more interested in money than in lives.

15

There were in consequence regular casualties below ground which could have been avoided with proper forethought.

He himself took the greatest care of the people who worked for him on all his estates, and thought that he would certainly see that his Coal Mine was properly supervised.

He knew at the same time that Daltry was cleverly persuading him by using arguments which he knew would specially appeal to him.

After arranging to meet Daltry and his Advisors at the Mine a week later, he had started to make plans immediately for the journey.

However when he went to visit his mother, she had a very different idea as to why he should be going into a part of the country she could never remember him visiting before.

"Can it be possible, Ervan," she asked, "that my prayers have at last been answered, and you intend to find yourself a wife?"

The Duke looked at her in astonishment.

"Why should you think that, Mama?"

"You told me you will be visiting the Marquess of Buxworth, who I hear, has a pretty daughter of exactly the right age."

"I do not know what you mean by 'exactly the right age', Mama," the Duke said defensively.

"I have always thought," his mother explained a little dreamily, "that a man, especially one like you, Ervan, should be a good deal older than his wife."

Her eyes were reminiscent as she said:

"Your father was twelve years older than I was and look how happy we were! I remember the first time I saw him, thinking that he was so handsome that he might have been a god from Olympus, and felt the same about him until his dying day!"

The way the Duchess spoke was very moving and the Duke said:

"Papa was very lucky to find you, Mama. But so far, I have never yet met a woman to whom I could for a moment, contemplate being married, so I remain a bachelor."

"I am very well aware of that!" the Duchess said sharply. "But, darling, you must be aware that you make a very attractive 4th Duke, and everybody admires you, but you should not forget that there must be a 5th and 6th, and a great number more after that."

The Duke laughed.

"You sound, Mama, as though I already have one foot in the grave, but I can only say, as I have not yet reached my twenty-ninth birthday, that there is plenty of time."

The Duchess sighed.

"That is always your answer, and I suppose in ten, twenty, thirty years' time you will be saying the same thing!"

The Duke laughed again.

"That is being very pessimistic, Mama, but perhaps I shall find the ideal wife on a peak of the Himalayas, sailing up the Amazon, or standing on top of the Acropolis in Athens!"

He nearly added:

"Or at the bottom of a Coal Mine!"

Then he thought that not only would his mother think it very unfunny, but he would have revealed to her the purpose of his journey North which he was anxious to keep secret.

The Duchess was an inveterate gossip, and the Duke knew that everything he said to her, especially where it concerned marriage, would be repeated to all her special friends and would ripple out like a stone thrown into the middle of a still pond.

"I cannot quite understand. . ." the Duchess was saying.

"What can you not understand, Mama?"

"Why, with all your charm and in view of all the glamorous women you have met and who have pursued you relentlessly, you have never yet fallen in love."

"I would not go so far as to say that, Mama!" the Duke said with a twist to his lips.

"I am talking about proper love," the Duchess said sharply, "not those '*affaires de coeur*' about which I hear far too much!"

"You should not listen!" the Duke replied automatically.

At the same time he was reflecting that anything he did was immediately related to his mother.

He often thought that almost before he had begun what she called an '*affaire de coeur*' she was aware of it, and was kept informed of every move even, he told himself, every kiss, almost before it happened.

He sat down beside the sofa on which his mother was reclining and took her hand in his.

"I love you, Mama," he said, "and although I want to please you, I can only say the reason why I am not married is entirely your fault!"

"My fault?" she asked. "When I have begged you almost on my knees to find yourself a wife!"

"I know, Mama, but when I compare the women I meet with you, I know they will not only disappoint me, but would undoubtedly bore me stiff within a few months."

Although the Duke was flattering his mother, which she greatly enjoyed, there was a great deal of truth in what he was saying.

The Duchess had not only been one of the most beautiful members of society when she married his father, but she had also become a legend in her own lifetime.

Royalty, Statesmen, Politicians, everybody, important or unimportant, adored the Duchess of Marazion.

She had a charm that made every man who met her her slave, and she was equally, although it seemed unbelievable, adored by women.

Looking back, the Duke thought that the reason was that it was impossible to be jealous or envious of a woman who was so warm-hearted and who gave so much of herself to everybody she met.

And she had so obviously been so happy with her husband that wherever they were they seemed to exude happiness and make it infectious.

What the Duchess had, which was different from most other people, was the capacity to make whoever she was speaking to feel that they were not only the most important people present as far as she was concerned, but also believe they were interesting and intelligent.

The dullest man blossomed into a wit when the Duchess talked to him, the plainest woman would sparkle, and in her own way have a beauty she had never had before.

It was a quality which the Duke had never found in anybody else, and he thought that his mother was truly unique and it would be impossible for him ever to find a woman who could compare with her.

Inevitably after the first physical rapture his *affaires* quickly began to fade and become a bore.

Now looking at him the Duchess thought almost despairingly that she understood exactly what he was saying.

Like his father before him, he was looking for perfection, something incomparable, in the same way that he so often set himself a challenge.

"I knew you were different from any other woman I had ever met," the 3rd Duke had said to the young daughter of an impoverished Baronet he had met out riding.

His future bride had been mounted on that occasion by her host with whom she was staying for the Hunt Ball.

She was contending with remarkable expertise with a spirited horse which was far better bred than anything her father could afford.

The excitement of it had brought a flush to her white skin and her eyes were sparkling.

Although her habit was old and not particularly well-cut, to the Duke seeing her for the first time she was the embodiment of everything that was beautiful, everything that had been in his dreams.

It had been genuinely love at first sight, and yet almost unbelievably the girl, who was literally '*Cinderella*', had hesitated before she had accepted him.

"You are too grand, too important," she had said when he proposed to her in a shabby, untidy room of the Manor House where she lived with her father, with only two very old servants to look after them.

"What does that matter when I love you?" the Duke had asked, "And I know you love me!"

"How do you know that?"

"I can see it in your eyes," he had said simply, "and I can feel your vibrations responding to mine as they did the first moment I spoke to you when we were out hunting."

"Without an introduction!" she had said with a smile.

"How could it possibly matter whether we were introduced or not," the Duke had replied, "when I recognised you the moment I looked at you?"

She knew what he was saying because she had felt the same. He had been in her dreams, she thought, ever since she was a child. Then suddenly he was there, looking magnificent on the finest horse she had ever seen, smiling at her in a way which made her heart turn a dozen somersaults.

Although it was a dull day her eyes seemed to be blinded by the sunshine.

Thinking back into her memories the Duchess's fingers unconsciously tightened on her son's.

Then as she looked at him, knowing how much he resembled his father and at the same time herself, she said just as if she had been speaking her memories aloud:

"That is what I want for you!"

"And what I want too," the Duke replied, "but, Mama, it has not yet happened to me, and perhaps it never will!"

The Duchess had sighed.

"In which case I can only go on praying."

20

"Of course!"

There was a little silence. Then in a different tone the Duchess asked:

"What are you doing about that red-haired creature who everybody tells me is 'Medusa' in a modern dress?"

The Duke threw back his head and laughed.

"If anybody in the *Beau Monde* could hear you, Mama, they would be horrified! The Princess is noted as being the most beautiful woman in Vienna!"

"She is noted for a lot of other things as well!" was the tart reply. "Let me remind you, Ervan, Austrian husbands are very touchy about their honour."

"That is what I have heard too," the Duke answered, "so you will be relieved to hear, Mama, that the Princess is leaving England tomorrow in order to meet her husband in Paris."

"And not a day too soon!" the Duchess commented.

"She is very alluring," her son replied, "and I will not hear a word against her."

There was a faint smile on his lips as he was thinking that it had been one of the most fiery and in a way most exciting affairs in which he had ever taken part.

The Princess had enticed him deliberately and with a determination which he could only admire.

She was sophistication personified: a woman whose desires could out-run a man's, and was, the Duke found, never satisfied.

He would not have been the hero so many people admired if he had not been wholly masculine and very much a man in other aspects besides his athletic achievements.

Because he seldom thought about himself in that way, he had no idea how many women sighed after him and dreamt of him as they slept beside their dull, complacent husbands who lacked the fire they sensed in the Duke, and which to him was as natural as the air he breathed.

Of course he was aroused by beautiful women and ready to accept the favours of those who made it very clear that they thought he was the most handsome and exciting man they had ever met.

But this had nothing to do with the ideal which lay hidden in his heart, an ideal engraved on his mind from the moment he became aware that his father and mother loved each other to distraction.

Because of this he had been encompassed since his birth by a love which coloured his thoughts, his feelings and, if he thought about it, his very soul.

Because his parents, while they seemed to him so god-like, were also very human, he could remember their laughter which was also part of his childhood's happiness.

He could laugh now with his mother and assure her that yet another *affaire* was over, burnt out as quickly as it had been kindled.

"Then why, if you are not interested in his daughter, are you going to visit the Marquess of Buxworth?" the Duchess demanded.

"He has some horses I want to see, and so has D'Arcy Armitage," the Duke had replied.

"Horses!" the Duchess exclaimed scornfully. "Do men ever think about anything else?"

"Occasionally, Mama, which is what you have just been complaining about!"

The Duchess was forced to laugh before she said: "Then all I can say, dearest, is that I am glad to hear the last of the Princess! I am just wondering who will take her place."

"I am wondering the same thing!" her son replied provocatively and his mother slapped his hand.

Sitting comfortably now in front of the fire the Duke wondered what he would feel if he was returning home after his visit to tell a wife his impressions of a Coal Mine, and to ask her opinion as to whether he should or should not buy it.

Then he told himself, it was not the sort of question in which any of the women he had ever known would be remotely interested.

22

Any conversation he had with them was invariably concerned with nothing but himself and the Lady to whom he was speaking.

Anything outside that particular golden island on which they found themselves was of so little consequence that it was impossible to pursue it.

"What do women really think about?" the Duke had once asked one of his closest friends, who replied:

"Where you are concerned, Ervan – only love!"

That, the Duke admitted, was perfectly all right for an evening, a night, or perhaps some very special day when, although it was unusual, he and a woman were alone together.

But if he had to talk of love at breakfast, luncheon, dinner and tea, and all through the night he knew it would be too much – much, much too much!

He had the frustrating feeling that whatever conversation he started with a woman always got back, sooner rather than later, to the question of their feelings for each other

"In which case, what is the point of being married," he asked quite reasonably, "if for an intellectual and stimulating conversation I have to go to the Club as I do now, or invite my men-friends to a bachelor dinner?"

There was no answer to this, and he told himself to stop being introspective and to enjoy life, which as far as he was concerned was indeed very enjoyable.

The Proprietor came into the parlour to inform him that dinner was ready, and he was followed by two buxom young women wearing mob-caps.

They both looked spotlessly clean, the Duke noted, and had doubtless taken extra trouble with themselves as they were waiting on him.

The first course was soup which the Duke knew must have been made by Hanson after his own particular recipe.

Because he was hungry he finished every drop in the tureen.

The next course was leg of lamb, a little over-cooked but edible.

After it, came stuffed pigeon turned on a spit with pepper and salt thrown onto it, until it was cooked exactly to his liking.

The Duke did full justice to all these dishes, but only took a very little of the trifle which was heavily laced with sherry, and two or three mouthfulls of the cheese which brought an end to the meal.

He accepted a glass of brandy which having been kept for some years was rather better than the claret.

Congratulating the Landlord, he moved from the table, which was then cleared by the maids, to sit once more in front of the fire.

He had not been there long before he began to feel sleepy, and he thought that if the fog had cleared by the morning he would want to leave very early.

Therefore the best thing he could do was to go upstairs to bed.

While eating his dinner he had made enquiries as to whether by chance there had been any sign of his brake and his other servants.

The Landlord shook his head.

"Three other travellers 'ave asked for accommodation owing to the fog, Sir, an' it's reel glad we are to see 'em."

He gave a deep belly-laugh before he added:

"They all sez round 'ere it's an ill wind that blows nobody any good, but fog's better for business than wind any day of th' week!"

He went from the room laughing loudly at his own joke, and the Duke hoped that if the fog cleared his servants would catch up with him tomorrow morning.

Anyway there was no need to worry about them. When they arrived at the Marquess of Buxworth's house they would be told he was not there and would go on to Lord D'Arcy Armitage's.

As he walked up the stairs he heard two men talking in

the Public Dining-Room and had a glimpse of a woman who had her back to him.

She was still eating, and he thought it was likely that because the Landlord had been so busy with the Duke's dinner the other guests had been forced to wait for theirs.

It was only a passing thought and as he went into his bedroom he was thinking once again of his rendezvous with Captain Daltry, and wondering if he and his associates had also been inconvenienced by the fog.

Hanson had left everything ready for him.

His silk nightshirt was warming on a chair in front of the fire, and beside it was a long velvet robe which his valet always packed for him when he was travelling.

If his bedroom was cold, which it often was in Country Houses, he found he appreciated the extra warmth of it.

He undressed, threw his evening-clothes on a chair, and put on his nightshirt and the velvet robe to sit down in front of the fire.

There was he thought, something very cosy about a fire which could transform the most ordinary, unattractive bedroom into something warm and welcoming.

He remembered that because his mother had known how much he liked it, he was always allowed a fire when he was a child, and also when he was a boy.

He had often been bitterly cold at School in the winter, and he would come home for the holidays to find a fire in his bedroom which was a joy he had never forgotten.

He supposed the cold and the experience of suffering every possible discomfort together with the other boys at School had made him tough enough to do all the things in which he had excelled as he grew older.

"Soft living makes a man soft!" a soldier had said to him once.

Although he disliked discomfort for discomfort's sake, the Duke had to agree that there was something in what he said.

He had the idea that the trains would add to the softness of the British people.

Men would travel in them and therefore not be exercising their muscles by riding or enduring the inclemency of the elements.

'Whatever happens,' the Duke thought, 'we must not grow soft as a nation!'

He wondered if that should be a reason for him not to develop the digging of more coal but to concentrate as he was at the moment on the breeding of fine horses.

Then he told himself nobody could stop progress. It was something that had been going on since the beginning of time, when primitive man had first discovered the wheel.

"Barrows, carts, carriages and now trains! What will come after that?" the Duke asked himself.

He remembered there was ballooning at Vauxhall Gardens and thought perhaps the next step would be something to do with the sky.

The he told himself he was being imaginative and the best thing he could do was to get into bed and go to sleep.

He rose to his feet and as he did so there was a knock on the door that was so soft he could hardly hear it, and when he did not reply but waited for it to come again the door opened.

It was not the door onto the passage by which he had entered the room but another door he had noticed on one side of the bed and which he knew led into the empty bedroom he had reserved next to his own.

In old Inns such as this most of the bedrooms communicated with each other, and another reason why the Duke always liked the rooms on either side of him to be empty was that the doors were usually badly fitted.

Now as the door opened – and it flashed through his mind he should have checked that it was bolted – a young woman came in.

She had fair hair hanging loose on either side of her face and over her shoulders, and she was wearing, the Duke saw, a pretty blue wollen dressing-gown which fastened down the front and had a small collar trimmed with lace.

He stared at her in astonishment.

Then as she looked at him and he expected she would retreat immediately with a murmured apology for intruding, she came into the bedroom and pulled the door shut behind her.

"Please," she said, "would you . . mind very much if I . . stayed here with you for . . a minute or two?"

She saw the suprise on the Duke's face and added quickly:

"It is just that I . . think a man is . . going to try to get into my bedroom and I do not . . know what else to . . do."

"What man?" the Duke asked automatically. "Do you mean a traveller?"

The girl, for she was little more, moved towards him until she was standing beside him in front of the fire.

Then she said in a low voice:

"He spoke to me downstairs . . and although I tried to be very cold and . . haughty he sat down at my table . . and offered me a glass of port!"

She spoke quite quietly and calmly, but the Duke was aware that there was an expression of fear in her eyes and her fingers as she spoke were entwining themselves in each other.

"Then what happened?" he asked.

"I had not quite . . finished my meal," she said, "but because I did not wish to become . . involved with him I . . rose from the table and . . said 'goodnight'."

"Did he reply?"

"He did not stand up, but merely said as I moved away:

" 'I shall be with you in a few minutes!' "

The girl drew in her breath. Then as the Duke did not speak she went on:

"For a moment I felt very frightened. Then when I reached my room I thought I would lock myself in and there would be no reason to be afraid."

"Was that impossible?"

"There is a lock," the girl said, "but it is not very firmly

27

fixed and I think a man could quite easily, if he . . wanted to . . push the . . door open."

She paused before she went on:

"It was . . foolish of me . . but I did not think of that . . not until I was undressed. Then I heard his voice . . talking to another man with whom he was driving."

Her fingers twisted themselves together even more as she went on:

"It was then I became really . . afraid of what might . . happen and seeing the . . communicating door I thought I would . . hide."

"So you went into the room next to mine!"

"Yes. But when I saw the light under your door, I knew you would . . help me."

"How did you know that?" the Duke enquired.

"I saw you when you came . . downstairs to . . dinner."

"And having seen me for that brief moment you thought you could trust me?"

She gave a smile that seemed somehow to illuminate her face as she said:

"You look . . like a . . Royal."

It was the first time she had looked at him without fear in her eyes, and after a moment the Duke said in a puzzled voice:

"You mean you thought I was a Prince or a King?"

The girl gave a little chuckle.

"No, I did not mean that, not that sort of Royal but one with twelve points."

"You mean a stag!" the Duke exclaimed, knowing that a stag with twelve points on his horns was referred to as a 'Royal'.

Again the girl was smiling and he thought there was something rather attractive and elfin-like about her.

"I suppose I should explain to you," she said, "that I often see people as . . animals and the man who is pursuing me is definitely an ugly and dangerous . . stoat!"

The Duke laughed. Then as he did so the girl put her

finger to her lips and he found himself listening as she was.

The wooden floor of the passage outside was uncarpeted and they could hear footsteps.

Then in the distance there was a sharp knock.

The Duke knew then that not only were he and the girl listening but also the man who had knocked.

The knock came again, then there was a sound of somebody raising the latch several times.

It was followed a few seconds later by a subdued crash as if the man had put his shoulder to the door, then having forced it ajar opened it as quietly as possible.

Now, as the girl looked up at the Duke, he saw that she was very pale and her eyes were wide and frightened.

"How . . can this . . h.happen?" she asked. "I had . . no idea a man would . . do such a thing!"

Because she looked so pale and the Duke could see that she was trembling he said:

"Sit down, you are quite safe here and I will see that he does not harm you."

He thought as he spoke that he should go out into the passage and tell the man what he thought about him.

Then after consideration he decided it would be a mistake and the less fuss that was made the better in the girl's interests.

If the room was empty there would be no point in the intruder staying there for very long.

"You are quite safe," he repeated in a quiet voice, "and when he has gone we will make sure he does not disturb you again."

"Thank you . . thank you! I knew I could . . trust you to . . help me."

"I am flattered that I should have given you that impression," the Duke said. "But surely you should not be travelling alone? Or have you got lost in the fog?"

"I was waiting for the Stage-Coach at the cross-roads," she said, "about three miles away. Then when it did not come, and the fog which has been hanging about all day

29

grew worse, I walked here knowing that when the coach did arrive the travellers on it would, if it was early, have something to eat while they changes horses, and if it was late, stay the night."

"So the Stage-Coach is lost in the fog!" the Duke commented. "I am not suprised. But where are you going - and alone?"

"To London."

"To London?" the Duke repeated. "That is a long way, but surely somebody should have accompanied you?"

She turned her face towards the door and he had the feeling she was blushing as she said:

"It may seem very . . reprehensible . . but actually there was no one that I could ask to . . come with me."

The way she said it made the Duke remark slowly and perceptively:

"I think you are running away!"

She did not reply, and after a moment he asked:

"Is it from School? Because if so, I must take you back."

"No, it is not from School," she said quickly. "And it is nothing to do with you. I shall be quite all right if I might just stay here until that . . man has . . gone."

"Suppose tomorrow night and the night after that there are other men like him?" the Duke suggested.

She turned her face to stare at him, her eyes very wide.

"But surely . . all men are not like that? After all . . he has never seen me before . . tonight."

The Duke wanted to smile at the innocence of the remark but instead he said somewhat severely:

"No decent young woman would ever travel alone. Although you may be perfectly safe on the Stage-Coach because there will be other women to whom you could appeal for assistance, things like this do happen, and as far as I can make out you are in an Inn alone with three strangers – all men!"

"But you are . . different!"

"So you are kind enough to tell me. At the same time I

might easily be another stoat like the man who has just burst into your room."

She shook her head and gave a little laugh.

"No, you are a Royal! I knew it the moment I saw you!"

"That is something I am delighted to be," the Duke said. "But please explain to me why you see people as animals?"

As she smiled he realised she had a dimple in her right cheek.

"I draw them like that."

"Draw?"

She gave a little sigh.

"I am determined to be an artist. That is why I am going to London. I am quite certain that if I can find somebody to teach me or I can join an Art Class, I could sell my pictures and keep myself."

"Why should you want to do that?"

"Because I am sick of being ordered about and told I have to do things I do not want to do! Although it is misery to leave my horses behind, I simply have to be independent!"

"But that is impossible for a woman."

"Why should it be?" she asked fiercely. "Men are allowed to do what they want to do, but women are restricted, constrained, confined and bullied. There is no other word for it, they are bullied from the moment they are born."

She spoke so violently and at the same time looking so small and frail, and with her hair falling over her shoulders, so young and feminine, that the Duke wanted to laugh.

"Now listen," he said, "you have to be sensible about this."

"Why should I?"

"Because you cannot wander about the world looking as you do, and avoid being insulted by the type of man who approached you downstairs."

"It is unfair that there should be one law for men and another for women!"

"I think women have said that since the beginning of

time," the Duke said, "but there is nothing you can do about it."

The girl sighed.

"First one is bullied by one's father," she said, "then by one's husband. How can I ever be myself and lead my own life unless I am rich enough to be beholden to nobody?"

"However rich you may be," the Duke retorted, "you cannot look after yourself and be alone at your age."

"I think you are wrong, and I intend to prove it."

He did not speak for a moment. Then he said:

"Try going back to your bedroom, and facing whoever is waiting there for you?"

There was a touch of fire in her eyes as she replied:

"That is unfair and unsporting, and in fact you are breaking all the Queensberry Rules and hitting below the belt!"

The Duke laughed.

"Forgive me, but I was only trying to prove my point, that you need somebody to look after you."

"Would it really make things better if I had some tiresome old woman with me, fussing like an old mother hen?"

"Yes, of course it would! You would be chaperoned, and strange men would not dare to speak to you!"

"The whole thing is ridiculous!"

"I did not make the social rules," the Duke replied, "and I do not think you have the power to unmake them."

"Then what can I do?" she asked helplessly.

"Go home, and do not run away again until you can plan things better and at least ensure that you do not get marooned in a fog!"

"That is something I cannot do . . or rather . . have no intention of doing."

"In which case," the Duke said, "Royal or no Royal, I presume I shall have to wash my hands of you!"

She looked at him apprehensively.

"What are you . . going to do?"

"Personally I wish to go to bed," the Duke said, "and the only suggestion I can make is that you can, if you wish, occupy the empty room through which you came, or there is another on the other side of mine which I engaged so that I could be quiet and sleep – undisturbed!"

She smiled as he said the last word before she replied:

"I promise you I do not snore, and I move about very quietly."

She paused before she added:

"Incidentally, I am very, very grateful, and you are just as kind as I thought you would be!"

"That is all very well," the Duke replied, "but now I feel somewhat responsible for you. After all, this may happen again tomorrow night."

She gave a little cry.

"No, no! You would not be there!"

"Then – go home!"

There was a long silence and he knew she was thinking over very carefully what he had said.

"I . . I cannot do . . that," she said at length.

"Why not?"

He knew as he watched her face while she tried to find an answer to his question that she was not going to tell him the truth.

Chapter Two

The Duke waited.

Then as if she suddenly thought of a way in which she could change the conversation, the girl said:

"I would like to show you something to explain why I am going to London, and have your opinion on it."

The Duke raised his eye-brows and she went on:

"It is some drawings and paintings I have done, and they are in my bedroom."

She looked towards the communicating door and the Duke was aware that she was frightened of going back to her room.

"I will fetch them," he said. "Where are they?"

"They are in a canvas bag propped against the chair in the window."

The Duke rose from his chair.

"Before we go any further," he said, "I think you should tell me your name."

"Ilitta . . Calvert."

There was a distinct pause before she gave her surname and he knew she was wondering whether it would be a mistake to tell the truth in case he knew any of her relatives.

He did not say anything, but opened the door into the empty room he had engaged, and leaving it open so that he was guided by the light from his own room, he opened a door opposite which he knew must lead into Ilitta's bedroom.

As he expected, by this time the man who was pursuing her had given up the chase.

34

But the door into the passage was open, and he found as he had expected, that the lock was broken.

The Duke's lips tightened as he thought how unpleasant it was for any woman, whatever her age or class, to be insulted in such a manner by a stranger.

He was well aware it happened frequently, and older and more respectable Ladies invariably blamed the woman in question.

The Duke was sure it was often unfair, but the argument was quite simple: no woman who valued her virtue and reputation would put herself in the position where a man could approach her so unpleasantly.

Looking across the room, which was quite small, the Duke saw there was a hand-grip in which he supposed Illita had packed her clothes.

It was open on the floor and beside it propped against the chair, as she said, was a large flat canvas bag.

He picked it up, and as he did so was aware of a sweet, fresh fragrance which reminded him of spring flowers.

He assumed that most young women travelling alone would not be able to afford to buy perfume.

But he was sure from Ilitta's appearance, even though he had only seen her in a dressing-gown, that she was not poverty-stricken.

Then why, he asked himself, was she travelling alone to London, determined to earn her own living?

There was an obvious answer: her clothes had been a present from some ardent admirer, perhaps her lover, who had now left her without providing adequately for her future.

However experienced as he was with women, the Duke was quite certain that Ilitta was very innocent and inexperienced.

She had undoubtedly been truthful when she said she had not expected a man who had never seen her before to approach her after she had retired to her bedroom.

"The last thing I want to do is to become involved in her

problems," the Duke told himself. "She must go home. It is the only thing she can do!"

He thought cynically that it was part of the new ideas current among some of the younger generation that a girl, even if she was a Lady, should think of earning money rather than concentrate on getting married to a man who would look after her and provide for her.

Once again he told himself it was progress. At the same time, it was something, in his opinion, to be deprecated and certainly not encouraged.

He walked back again to his own room and knew that Ilitta was pleased when she saw what he was carrying.

Then she asked a little nervously:

"Had that . . man been in . . my room?"

"He has broken the lock," the Duke replied, "and the door was therefore open."

Ilitta gave a little cry. Then she said:

"Thank you . . thank you . . for letting me stay with you! If you had refused I would have been . . very frightened!"

"And rightly so," the Duke observed. "Therefore as this sort of thing may happen again and again, the sooner you are sensible and return home, the better!"

He saw a flash of defiance in her eyes and she parted her lips to start arguing with him. Then instead she said:

"Please let me show you my drawings. I have a feeling, although I may be mistaken, that you have a knowledge of Art."

It might have been a bold venture, but it was in fact very perceptive of her.

The Duke was a patron of the Royal Academy, and because his own collection was famous the Queen frequently consulted him about pictures she wished to buy for Buckingham Palace or Windsor Castle.

The Duke had also advised Her Majesty and the Prince Consort on which of the modern artists they should choose to paint their portraits.

Every time that they consulted him, they had been

extremely pleased with the artist he had recommended.

Now as Ilitta put the canvas bag he had given her down on the hearth-rug in front of the fire and crouched down beside it, the Duke settled himself in the only armchair in the room.

It was worn and creaked under his weight, but as he crossed his legs and sat back he looked very comfortable.

Ilitta drew out a small canvas.

Then before she passed it to him she said:

"I want you to be completely and absolutely truthful! If you think I have no talent for painting, then please say so."

The Duke, who had seen a number of water-colours which it was fashionable for Ladies of leisure to do pass the time, had always thought that amateurs should leave art to the professionals and find something else to do.

Now he was quite certain that what he would see would be work which if in oils, would be a messy composition and if a water-colour indifferently drawn.

He put out his hand without speaking and Ilitta handed him the canvas saying as she did so:

"That is my horse. I have had him since he was a foal and I love him more than anybody else in the whole world!"

The Duke found himself looking at a small, but remarkable painting of a young horse.

The main point of the composition was the vigour that he could sense in the way the horse was moving. And this surprised him because it was so unusual.

Portraits of animals were traditionally poised and stiff and painted, as humans were, as if they had a stick to support their spines.

It was difficult to think of them doing anything except staring stiffly out of the canvas.

Ilitta's horse on the contrary was just breaking into a gallop, and the Duke could feel that the animal was sensing his freedom after being cooped up in his stable and was longing to stretch his legs.

Every muscle seemed to be strained for the speed with which he intended to move.

The Duke did not speak. He only looked at the picture, knowing there were mistakes in the painting which of course were due to inexperience.

At the same time he was aware that Ilitta had captured movement on canvas which was rare and almost unique.

He did not say anything, but merely held out his hand and Ilitta gave him another canvas.

This was altogether different.

It was a study of rabbits in a wood, and it was obvious that two of them were suddenly alert to danger.

They were sitting up tense and ready in a split second to scamper away, while the others were for the moment blissfully unaware of what was about to happen.

It was a clever idea, and the sunlight percolating through the branches of the trees and turning the bark to gold was skilfully done.

Again the Duke held out his hand and Ilitta said:

"Thoses are the only two canvases I have with me. The other pictures I have painted and which I would have liked to bring with me were framed by one of my Governesses and it seemed a pity to remove them from where they were hung."

"You have nothing else?" the Duke enquired.

He was speaking for the first time since Ilitta had given him the pictures.

She looked down at the canvas bag.

"You may be . . surprised at what else I have . . brought with me."

The Duke smiled.

"I enjoy being surprised!"

"Very well, but perhaps I should explain," she said. "What I have here are portraits which I have done, of course secretly, of people I have seen or who have been guests at my home."

She pulled out a piece of thick drawing-paper and handed it to the Duke.

Now he understood exactly what she meant when she said she thought of him as a stag.

What she had drawn was a caricature.

But while the man in question was in evening-dress, which was quite well sketched, his head was that of a fox-hound.

It was skilfully drawn, and the Duke thought that if he had ever met the man he would have recognised him, although the dog's head was undoubtedly copied from life.

Ilitta did not ask for his approval, and merely handed him another drawing. This was of an elderly man with a large paunch and ill-fitting clothes, and who had the head of a benign, rather ageing bull.

It was brilliant and at the same time very funny, and the Duke laughed aloud. As if the sound relieved the tension that Ilitta was feeling, she said quickly:

"You are . . not shocked?"

"Of course not. It is very clever! How on earth did you learn to do anything like this?"

"I have not been taught, that is the trouble," Ilitta said. "I begged Papa to let me have proper drawing lessons, but he said it was a waste of money."

She spoke bitterly and the Duke said:

"I hardly think you need very much teaching."

"But of course I do!" Ilitta contradicted sharply. "I am well aware that my paintings are not good enough and, although I draw what I feel and see, I am sure that technically I have a great deal to learn."

"And when you have done so – what then?"

Ilitta smiled.

"When I say I would like to sell my pictures it is not quite true. It would only be to pay a Drawing Master. However I would like to feel that I am doing something worthwhile. I mean if I can portray on canvas the animals I love and which mean so much to me, perhaps it will encourage people to worry more about cruelty to horses, and especially to the animals they shoot just for amusement."

The Duke looked at her in consternation.

"You are not one of those new thinkers," he asked, "who I hear are ranting against the killing of animals as if they were Buddhists, and think the whole population should eat grass!"

Ilitta laughed.

"No, not as bad as that," she said. "It is just that if an animal is killed for a reasonable purpose, then it must be done humanely and causing as little pain as possible. I do not think it matters if any of us die, because death is immaterial. What is wrong is suffering and pain! An animal or a bird that is wounded suffers in the same way as we do."

The Duke looked down at the pictures he was holding on his knee. Then he said:

"I follow your argument. At the same time there are different sorts of suffering. I wonder if you have considered what these men you have sketched so skilfully and somewhat cruelly would think if they saw the way in which you have portrayed them?"

"People have been lampooned and made fun of by the Cartoonists since the days of George IV."

"I am aware of that," the Duke said, "but I do not expect they enjot it."

"But I only draw men who should be taught the error of their ways!"

"In your judgement!" the Duke said a little sarcastically.

"Now you are being unkind," Ilitta said quickly, "and I suppose you are going to tell me I am wasting my time."

"I could not in honesty say anything of the sort!"the Duke replied. "I am astonished by your drawings, and find it hard to believe it when you say you have had no instruction and have not been assisted in way by a professional artist."

Ilitta stared at him.

"Are you saying you think they are good?"

"Very good indeed, in fact outstanding!"

For a moment she still stared as if she thought he was teasing her.

Then she clasped her hands together and said:

"I cannot believe it! Are you really saying this to me?"

"I think your picture of the horse is a brilliant effort to depict movement, and the same applies to the study of the rabbits. I am just a little nervous of the way you use your talent on human beings!"

Ilitta smiled, and it seemed to illuminate her face as if there was a light inside her.

"I have told you that I see you as a Royal, and what could be more complimentary than to be likened to the King of the Moors?"

"I appreciate that," the Duke said. "At the same time, you are a woman and nobody of importance will like being made to look a fool by a member of the weaker sex!"

There was a sudden flash in Ilitta's eyes, and he knew she wanted to argue with him.

Instead she drew out another piece of drawing-paper from her canvas bag and the Duke saw that this time it was a study of a woman.

One glance told him that she had been devastatingly critical in her own inimitable manner.

The woman was exquisitely dressed in the latest fashion, her full skirt billowing out from a tiny waist, her lace bertha falling softly over her sloping shoulders.

But on the long, swan-like neck there was the head of a cat!

It was a cat with a woman's eyes and a woman's lips parted provocatively. There was greed, jealousy and a very feline expression of desire for revenge portayed in the face which at the same time contrived to be very attractive.

It was so cruel and yet so clever that the Duke thought he must be looking at a cartoon by Gillray or Rowlandson.

He found it impossible to believe that anybody as young as Ilitta could possibly have drawn anything so remarkable.

41

Then it flashed through his mind that perhaps he had been decieved, and that because he was noted as a Patron of the Arts Ilitta was really an actress who had been paid to enlist his interest on behalf of an artist who had hitherto passed unnoticed.

Then he reasoned that nobody could possibly have been aware that there would be a fog or that he would stay at this particular Inn.

Besides he had only to look at Ilitta to know that she was not only what she appeared to be, but so transparently truthful that he felt as if he could read her thoughts.

He put down the picture of the woman with the head of a cat and asked:

"Have you anything more in 'Pandora's Box'?"

She shook her head.

"I came away in a hurry, and snatched up things I had just finished. Perhaps it was silly of me not to bring more."

"I think you have quite enough here to convince anybody in the world of Art that you have an exceptional talent."

"How can you say to me anything so wonderful?" Ilitta asked. "It is what I have been longing to hear, but everybody at home is so scathing about all my drawings that I began to doubt myself."

"Then you need not do that in the future," the Duke said. "But I think you are going the wrong way about it. You must persuade your father to let you go to London properly chaperoned, and get you the right sort of teacher."

He saw by the expression on Ilitta's face that she was quite certain this would never happen, and although he had meant to keep out of the whole problem he found himself saying:

"I am sure I can recommend the right person to teach you the points of technique you need to learn, in order to fulfil your talent."

"And you think I could . . sell my pictures?"

It flashed through the Duke's mind that any magazine would undoubtedly be prepared to accept her caricatures if she drew them of famous people.

They would cause a sensation, and although she would undoubtedly be ostracised socially she would certainly earn money if that was what she wanted.

Then he told himself that it would be very reprehensible for him to suggest anything like that to so young a girl.

He was moreover certain she was a Lady, and it would cause a great deal of trouble both for herself and for her family if she embarked on anything so provocative.

On the other hand her oil paintings could make her one of the new artists for whom he was always searching to exhibit their work in the Royal Academy.

At the last meeting he had said forcefully:

"I am sick to death of portraits of women who look like iced cakes, and of men so stiff with medals they would clank if they moved."

The other members had looked down their noses at his outburst.

"We must keep up our standards, Your Grace," one of them had said a little reproachfully.

"I am aware of that, Sir Joshua," the Duke replied. "But nothing can be more wearisome than seeing the same portraits by the same artists of the same people hanging on every wall! By all means, retain the traditional, but also open the doors to new ideas, new names which have not yet been allowed to cross the threshold."

He knew as he spoke that everybody would oppose him, simply because they clung jealously to what had always been done, and had no wish to strike out into the unknown.

Just as the Duke had always wanted to conquer mountains whose peaks had never previously been reached, and find the source of rivers that had never been discovered, so in everything else that interested him he wanted something new, something different, even though he was not quite certain himself what it might be.

He was thinking now how difficult it would be to help Ilitta to do anything unless she had the approval of her parents.

He felt she could not survive alone in London without that anymore than a frail canoe could steer itself down the Victoria Falls.

"What are you thinking?" she asked, and he knew she was trying to read his thoughts.

"I am thinking of you." the Duke answered truthfully, "and while I can say honestly and without exaggeration that you are quite exceptional as an artist, as a young woman of gentle birth you have to go home and find your way to London by a different route."

Ilitta did not answer.

She merely lifted her pictures, one by one, from the Duke's knee and put them back in her canvas bag.

Then without speaking she rose to her feet.

He looked at her and thought that with her fair hair falling over her shoulders and in her blue dressing-gown she seemed very young and, as if he had just realised it for the first time, very lovely.

He could understand how seeing her alone the man downstairs had desired her, and assumed she would be an easy conquest.

She had not the classical features which the Duke had always associated with beauty, and the majority of women he admired had not, being older, the frailty and slenderness of the girl standing in front of him.

She seemed insubstantial, ethereal, and at the same time when she smiled and showed her dimples there was something mischievous in her face which made her either very human or else elfin-like, he was not quite certain which.

Now in the silence she merely said:

"Thank you very much for being so kind to me, and for the encouraging things you have said."

"You are going back to your room?"

"I am sure you wish to sleep, and I shall be . . all right . . now."

44

There was a little tremor in the words which the Duke did not miss, and after a moment he said:

"I think as the lock on your door is broken you will find it hard to rest. May I therefore suggest that you move into this room and I will sleep next door?"

As he spoke he surprised himself.

It was not often that he was so unselfish, or went out of his way to assist somebody whom he had just met.

But somehow he felt protective towards this foolish child, who had already run into trouble and, if she continued in such a wayward manner, would run into a great deal more.

"No . . of course not," Ilitta said quickly. "I could not accept such a thing from you."

She paused, then added:

"But . . I should be grateful if I could . . sleep next door . . and perhaps there is a key or a bolt to the door."

"I am sure there is," the Duke agreed, "but I am perfectly prepared to let you stay here if you wish."

"You have been very kind," she said, "so kind that I am very thankful that when I came here you did not . . send me away."

"I would not think of doing such a thing!" the Duke said. "But I still beg of you to return to your home."

Ilitta looked away from him.

"I cannot do that," she said. "I promise you there is a very good reason why I must not go home at the moment."

The Duke had not moved from his chair and now, almost as though somebody was putting the idea into his mind, he felt it was as if it had been spoken in his ear.

"Do you see everybody you meet in the same penetrating manner in which you have portrayed the characters of those two men and the woman?" he asked.

"Usually I can," Ilitta replied. "But sometimes I have to force myself to see below the surface of the face they assume for outsiders."

She gave a little laugh and said:

"Yet without trying it is often most disconcerting."

She looked to see if the Duke was listening, then went on:

"But more often the idea comes to me quite instinctively and sometimes as I say in a most disconcerting manner. The other night I was talking to the man sitting next to me at dinner, and quite suddenly and unexpectedly I realised that he was a camel!"

She laughed again and it was a very young and joyous sound.

"I had never met a 'camel' before, except in the zoo, but there he was, sitting beside me, chewing in that funny way that camels do, and looking incredibly stupid!"

The way she spoke made the Duke laugh, and he said:

"I suppose you did not tell him of your discovery?"

"No, of course not!" Ilitta said. "I would not be so rude or so unkind! But I shall never be able to look at him in the future without thinking of him clopping across the desert sands!"

"I have an idea," the Duke said slowly, "which you may think impossible. In which case, I want you to say so immediately."

"What is it?"

She spoke unaffectedly and was obviously not nervous of anything he might suggest, and the Duke thought once again that this was something which showed how innocent she was.

An older woman would have been acutely aware of what he might be about to say to her.

Then as Ilitta looked at him enquiringly, her eyes very large in her pointed face, he said:

"I have a very important reason for coming to this part of the country. I have, in fact, been asked to do so by some men who wish to interest me in a financial proposition."

Ilitta did not speak, but sat down again on the hearth-rug at his feet, her face turned up to his.

Although the Duke was intent on what he was saying, he

noticed how the light from the fire brought out touches of the same colour in the fairness in her hair.

"I was just wondering if instead of going directly to London as you intended, you would come with me for the next two days. With your strange perception you could tell me if these men with whom I have had only a very brief acquaintance are people I can trust in matters of business."

"I understand what you are saying to me," Ilitta said, "and if you will trust me, I am quite certain I can help you."

She paused before she added:

"You may not like what you hear, but will realise I have to be completely and absolutely honest."

"That is what I want you to be," the Duke said, "and that is the reason why I have asked you to help me in this matter."

He thought as he spoke that most of his friends would not believe for a moment that he was interested only in Ilitta's powers of perception, rather than in her as a woman.

The thought struck him that if she accepted, as she obviously intended to do, he would have to make some explanation to Captain Daltry.

Then with his usual ability to find a solution quickly to any problem however complicated, he said:

"If you agree, I have an idea. You obviously cannot travel with me as yourself."

"Why not?" Ilitta asked.

He realised once again that the question was entirely innocent.

It had not struck her for a moment that he was a man who might behave towards her in the same way as the man from whom she had escaped.

He thought he should warn her once again that she was being reckless, then decided it would be a mistake.

When he had finished with her services, he would try again to persuade her to return home. If she refused, then he must leave her to go her own way, having of course rewarded her for anything she might have done for him.

He realised as he was thinking that Ilitta's eyes were on his face, and now she said:

"If I must not come with you as myself, then what do you suggest?"

"I was thinking that you look very young," the Duke repeated. "I have not seen you in your daytime attire, but I presume you wear your hair up and look a little older than you do at this moment."

"But of course!" Ilitta agreed. "I am over eighteen and it was only because I was in mourning until a month ago that I have not been to any grown-up parties or Balls."

That would account, the Duke thought, for why she seemed so childlike.

He also supposed that in this part of the country, which was sparsely inhabited and with few important houses, there would not be so many gaieties as there were for girls who lived nearer London.

"Then what I am going to suggest," he said aloud, "is that if you agree to travel with me tomorrow, you do so as my sister."

He smiled as he added:

"Actually I have a sister a little younger than you who is at school in Paris improving her French and doubtless learning a great deal about Art."

"She is very lucky!" Ilitta exclaimed. "I longed to go abroad and be educated, but of course Papa said it would be too expensive!"

The Duke thought that her father was probably a Country Gentleman living on a small estate, who would find the large bills for his daughter to be educated abroad quite beyond his means.

"Nobody where we will be going will have met my sister," he said, "or even knows she exists."

"It will be very exciting to pretend to be her," Ilitta replied, "and if you want me to look really young, perhaps I had better wear my hair as it is now."

"That is what I was going to suggest," the Duke agreed,

"but I doubt if anybody would question your identity, not to me at any rate!"

"Then . . perhaps you had better tell me your name," Ilitta said.

"Ervan Trecarron," the Duke replied. "I am a baronet."

"Then you come from Cornwall!"

"How do you know that?"

"I have read a great deal about Cornwall because it always sounds so interesting, and of course both Ervan and Trecarron are Cornish names."

"That is very perceptive of you, and as my sister's name is really Georgina we can say if anybody asks us, which is unlikely, that Ilitta is a nickname."

"You are being very clever!" she smiled, "but you must prevent me from making any mistakes."

"There is no reason why you should make any," the Duke answered, "and remember, Ilitta, these men know nothing about my private life, and quite frankly all they are interested in is my money."

Ilitta looked serious.

"Then we shall have to be very, very careful that they do not take it from you under false pretences."

"That is exactly why I am taking you with me," the Duke said. "I hope you will draw me pictures of them as animals, from which I shall be able to tell far more about them than anybody could explain in words."

Ilitta clapped her hands together.

"It all sounds a great adventure! Thank you, thank you for asking me to come with you!"

It struck the Duke once again that her attitude was really very reprehensible and somebody should stop her simply for the sake of her reputation.

Then he told himself that was none of his business.

It would doubtless be far worse for her to travel on alone to London knowing nothing of the world, and having not the slightest idea of how to protect herself.

'The only sensible thing she has done so far was to come

49

to me when she was in danger,' he thought. 'At the same time, if I had been a different sort of man, she might have been in an even more precarious position than she was with the man who broke down her door!''

He knew how shocked the Society Mamas, who chaperoned their daughters as if they were encircled with chain-armour, would be at the thought of a girl of eighteen sitting in his bedroom with both of them in their night attire.

They would not for one moment believe they were discussing Art.

They would put the worst possible construction on the fact that they were alone in an isolated Inn without any other woman in the place except for the servants.

'She ought not to be behaving in this preposterous manner,' the Duke thought and frowned.

Ilitta gave a little cry and asked:

"What is wrong? What has upset you?"

The Duke swept the frown from between his eyes and answered:

"Nothing important."

He knew as he spoke he should make one last attempt to persuade her to go home, but he knew if he did so he would miss what he thought of as a unique opportunity of sounding out Daltry by an original method which he was certain had never been thought of before.

He could not imagine what would happen if Ilitta with nothing to go on but her perception and her strange ability to capture a man or a woman's character with her pencil should denounce Daltry as a crook.

Then he thought such a thing was extremely unlikely and felt he was not taking much of a risk.

What most probably would happen would be that Ilitta would see Daltry as being greedy and asking more for the Coal Mine than its actual value.

"Whatever she says will undoubtedly be extremely helpful," he told himself.

50

Actually he was intrigued and amused by finding something so unexpected and strange in an Inn that he would never have visited in the normal course of events.

All his life the Duke had always followed his instinct when it came to exploration or seeking the unusual or original.

He knew now that those two adjectives were most applicable to Ilitta.

He glanced down at the canvas bag which was once again lying on the floor.

Then he wondered if it was the firelight or the fact that he was tired which had blinded him to the truth about her and if her drawing were really as brilliant as he had first thought.

But he felt sure he had not been deceived by what he had seen and in some way he could not determine at the moment he must certainly help Ilitta to persue her talent further.

Perhaps he could arrange a grant for her, from one of the Galleries he supported, or from one of the organisations of which he was a Patron.

He was much concerned with Art, Education, and opportunities for young people, and he was quite certain it would be easy for him to help her financially when he returned to London.

Once again while he was thinking deeply, Ilitta's eyes were on his face. Then as he smiled at her she said:

"You . . you are not . . regretting that you asked me?"

"No, of course not! I want you to come with me, but because we have a long way to go we must leave early in the morning."

"I will go to bed in the next room," Ilitta said. "If the Stage Coach arrives I shall be woken at six o'clock. But please, if it does not arrive, would you be kind enough, when you are called, to knock on my door?"

"Yes, of course," the Duke agreed

She rose to her feet and he rose too.

"What you must do," he said, "is to remove your belongings and put them in the next room and I will make certain all the doors are securely locked and bolted so that nobody can disturb you."

"Thank you," Ilitta said. "You are so kind that I cannot begin to tell you how grateful I am."

"The best way you can show me your gratitude," the Duke said dryly, "is to let us both have a good night's sleep. I have a feeling it is getting very late."

"I have kept you awake . . which was . . wrong of me."

She did not wait for his reply, but carrying her canvas bag ran through the door into the next room.

The Duke heard her pull open the door on the other side which led into the room she had occupied originally.

There were two candles alight by his bed and he carried one of them into the next room and set it down on the dressing-table.

As he did so Ilitta came back carrying her hand-grip and the gown she must have hung up in the wardrobe when she undressed.

As soon as she was in the room the Duke shut the door behind her.

He found there was a bolt on it, which fortunately had not been pushed home when she had come to him for his assistance.

He then bolted the door onto the passage and seeing that the lock was intact, turned the key.

"Now go to sleep," he said, "and do not worry about anything. I will make sure you are awoken in plenty of time so as not to keep me waiting. We will of course breakfast in my Private Parlour."

"You think of everything!" Ilitta exclaimed. "I will do exactly what you have told me, and try to go to sleep."

She smiled and he thought in the candlelight she looked rather like a small angel that had fallen out of Heaven by mistake.

Then as he went into his own room, closing the door

quietly behind him, he thought there was nothing angelic about the perceptiveness of her mind.

Unless her drawings were untrue, she had portrayed her victims so uncannily and so cynically that she might have been a middle-aged cartoonist with years of experience behind her.

"She is certainly very unusual," the Duke told himself as he got into bed.

Then he congratulated himself on having made a new discovery, one which might prove discomfiting to Daltry and his friends but, more important, would undoubtedly amuse and interest himself even more than the acquisition of a Coal Mine.

Chapter Three

The fog was clearing over the trees when the Duke drove his team carefully out of the Inn yard.

There was no sign of the sun, but Ilitta was certain it would break through the clouds later in the day.

She could hardly believe it was true when she was awoken by a knock on her door and heard the Duke's voice say:

"It is nearly six o'clock and I shall be having breakfast in a quarter-of-an-hour."

She jumped up, excited at the idea of going with him, and realised as she did so that she had slept peacefully.

She thought of what had happened last night before he had saved her and felt herself shiver.

Then she told herself there was no point in remembering unpleasant things and today was going to be an adventure she had never envisaged.

She put on the gown in which she had travelled and packed the one she had changed into for dinner.

She had never travelled alone or for that matter stayed in anything except a very grand or respectable Hotel once or twice in her life.

She therefore had no idea that wearing an evening-gown of any sort constituted, because she was alone, an invitation to any man who was out for a 'little bit of fun'.

Now she remembered she was to be Sir Ervan's sister and having parted her hair down the centre, brushed it until it seemed to dance with a life of its own.

She then tied it on each side of her head with blue ribbons.

She thought when she looked at herself in the mirror that she had stepped back five or six years and was sure because she was so slim that nobody would think she was grown up.

"That is what he wants," she told herself, "and it is very clever of him to make me his sister."

She hurried downstairs carrying her luggage in her hand and when she entered the Private Parlour the Duke felt as if she brought the sunshine with her.

He was already eating his breakfast, but he rose perfunctorily from his chair, then sat down again.

"Come on, Ilitta!" he said. "We have a long way to go and the sooner we are on our way the better!"

He spoke to her, Ilitta thought, just as a brother might have done.

Actually she was as anxious to get away as he was, hoping not to see again the man who had broken into her bedroom.

There was nobody about in the Inn when they left, with the exception of the Proprietor and an ostler from the stables who looked sleepy and disgruntled.

There was also no sign of the Stage-Coach which had been delayed last night.

It was a warm day for the end of September with just a few of the leaves on the trees beginning to turn brown, but when the sun came up the air was fresh and seemed almost spring-like.

Hanson sitting behind them was telling the Duke he had found there was a shorter way to their destination which would enable them to cut off several miles of their journey, and therefore to arrive almost at the time they were expected for the meeting with Captain Daltry.

The Duke who liked to be punctilious in everything, and disliked being late even if it was unavoidable, settled down to driving his team and making sure there were no unnecessary delays on the road.

Because they were in fact moving at what Ilitta felt must be a record speed, she tied the ribbons on her bonnet even more tightly and enjoyed the feel of the sun on her face and the beauty of the countryside.

Hanson had accepted the Duke's explanation while he dressed him that Ilitta was a distant cousin, to whom he was giving a lift, but that he intended to introduce her to Captain Daltry as his sister.

Having been with his master for some years Hanson was never surprised at anything that happened.

He merely thought to himself that Ilitta was unlike most of the other ladies in the Duke's life.

The Duke however was thinking as the sun rose in the sky that it was a good day for shooting partridges.

He wished he had stayed a little longer with his mother and arranged a day over the fields where he knew he had every chance of bagging a good number of birds.

He had made it clear when he inherited from his father that his mother could occupy the Dower House on every one of his estates.

Because these were numerous she had a large choice.

She had however chosen the Dower House near the Duke's mansion in Gloucestershire as well as the one in Cornwall.

It was at Marazion that she had spent the happiest days of her married-life and the Duke knew the reason why she seldom visited it now was that it brought back so many memories.

She still, after eight years of widowhood, missed his father unbearably.

Because he was aware that she was often lonely he persuaded her whenever possible to come to London, where because he was unmarried she acted as hostess at Marazion House in Grosvenor Square.

As she was still beautiful, and still had that charm which was ageless, the moment she arrived everybody from the Social World came to call on her.

They kept insisting that she gave another of her

famous parties, like those she had given in the old days when, as somebody said to her son:

"London would not have been the same without the Duchess standing at the top of the staircase and glittering like a constellation of stars."

The Duke had smiled at the compliment and when he remembered it afterwards he wondered how he could ever find a wife who would look so lovely or grace the family diamonds as his mother did.

Before he left Gloucestershire he had arranged that after staying with his friend D'Arcy Armitage he would go back to spend a few more days with his mother before proceeding to London, or wherever else his fancy took him.

'I suppose really I should go to Cornwall,' he thought.

He had not been there since the spring and of all his estates it was Marazion where he had spent the happiest days of his childhood.

On the other hand, because it was a long way for people to travel, he was often alone there and, although he disliked admitting it to himself, at times lonely.

He thought now, driving with Ilitta beside him, that the train service which was already being built to Falmouth would make it easier for his friends to accept his invitations.

Although he frowned at the idea of trains supplanting horses, he knew in his heart, since trains had carried race-goers to Epsom this year, it was a losing battle.

"Then why," his conscience asked, "are you buying a Coal Mine?"

The answer was quite simple: Captain Daltry had persuaded him into it almost against his inclinations.

He had begun to think of the reports of the Children's Employment Bill of three years earlier.

It had horrified the conscience of the country, and it certainly horrified him.

The descriptions of boys and girls employed together in the darkness of the Coal Mines, of women naked to the waist with chains between their legs crawling on all fours down tunnels under the earth, and drawing gigantic burdens, had been appalling.

He had been one of the first people to speak for Lord Ashley when he heard he was introducing a Bill to exclude all women and girls from the Pits and was delighted when he succeeded and was proclaimed a National Hero.

The Duke would certainly not employ in any Mine that he owned, men who were not strong enough to endure the inevitable discomfort of working underground.

What was more he was determined to have every possible safety device that was known to ensure that there were as few accidents as possible.

'I might even invent a few of my own,' he thought.

What might be necessary kept his mind occupied for a large number of miles.

It was only as the sun came out and the last vestige of the fog of the night before dispersed that he looked down at Ilitta with a smile to ask:

"Are you enjoying yourself?"

"I have never before driven behind such magnificent horses," she answered, "nor have I travelled so fast."

The Duke smiled.

It was what he wanted to hear. Then he said:

"We have another fifteen miles to go, but I reckon we should arrive before one o'clock, which is the time I am expected."

The place where he was to meet Captain Daltry was not very far from the Marquess of Buxworth's house, and had he stayed there last night as arranged, he had intended, before he left, to inspect the Marquess's stables, and have a quick look at his estate.

The Duke was always intensely interested in how other people were farming their land, and whether they had as many innovations as he had introduced, especially in Gloucestershire.

But while his estates were acclaimed as models of their

kind, and an example to every Landlord in England, he was still prepared to admit there was more he could learn, if only from other people's mistakes.

He wondered if he should ask Ilitta whether, since she came from this part of the country, she had met or heard of the Marquess.

He also played with the idea of telling her his real identity, then decided against it.

He was afraid that if he did so she might become self-conscious, as so many people were in his presence, which would sweep away the ease with which she talked to him now.

It was almost, he thought to himself, as if she actually was his sister rather than a young woman with an attractive man.

He knew it was because she was so innocent and unsophisticated that it apparently had never crossed her mind that she was in a position which dozens of women would envy in that she was spending a day in his company.

They were free from the social restrictions which in other circumstances would have made it impossible for them to talk to each other frankly or intimately.

He had made it very clear to Captain Daltry that he preferred to be known as 'Sir Ervan Trecarron' when he was inspecting the Mine.

"I am glad you said that, Your Grace," Captain Daltry replied, "because it was something I was going to suggest to you myself."

He paused as if he was feeling for words before he went on:

"You will understand that it would be the greatest mistake for anybody working in the Mine or living in the neighbourhood to be aware that it is up for sale."

"You think it might upset them?"

"Of course it would!" Captain Daltry ejaculated. "The ordinary working man would be afraid either that he might lose his job, or that a new employer would make heavy demands on him which he would find it difficult to meet."

"I see your point," the Duke said briefly.

"What is more," Captain Daltry went on, warming to his theme, "if the local reporters should have the idea that the Mine is up for sale or that anybody as important as Your Grace is thinking of buying it, it would be splashed all over the local newspapers and would undoubtedly be repeated in '*The Morning Post*' and '*The Times*'!"

The Duke could only agree that this would be a grievous mistake and Captain Daltry continued:

"It is therefore important that Your Grace should just appear to be an ordinary visitor to the neighbourhood, interested in local activities."

"Of course," the Duke murmured.

"The men I shall have with me," Captain Daltry went on, "waiting to show you the Mine will have no idea you have any other name."

"I am sure that is sensible," the Duke agreed.

"In order to make the whole thing seem more natural," Captain Daltry said, "I have arranged that we shall have luncheon at Mr. Newall's house, even though he is away. It is a large mansion, situated only about two miles from the village where the Mine is, and he has already expressed his deep regret that he cannot be there in person to entertain you."

It all sounded to the Duke as if the arrangements were exactly what he himself would prefer, and he merely told Captain Daltry that he would arrive just before one o'clock on Wednesday.

He had then written off to the Marquess of Buxworth and Lord Armitage inviting himself to stay.

Because Lord Armitage's house was in the South of the County he knew if he left there early in the morning, he would be able to be with his mother by dinnertime.

He accordingly arranged to send two changes of horses on the road by which he would travel.

Then having decided that the arrangements measured up

to his idea of perfect organisation he had set off, still determined to keep the real reason for his journey a secret.

Because he was so famous and aroused gossip whatever he did or wherever he went, he knew that to have everybody chattering about the possibility of his buying a Coal Mine would be to have dozens of offers of other Mines pouring in.

Worst of all, he would have coach-builders pleading with him to purchase a private train.

Since a Royal Railway Carriage had been made for the Queen, he was aware that already two of his contemporaries intended to travel, as they put it, 'under their own steam' as soon as there were railways connecting London with their homes in the North of England.

"I have always driven to stay with you," he said to the Earl of Derby who lived in Lancashire, "and I see no reason to change my ways."

"You must move with the times, Ervan," the Earl had replied, "and what is more, you must give us older fellows a lead."

He had laughed before he added:

"If you can climb to the top of the Matterhorn, you can hardly object to being a Pioneer in the new Era of Steam."

The Duke had told himself obstinately it was something he had no intention of ever doing.

He was therefore rather shaken when three years ago he learnt that after the Queen had taken her first train ride from Windsor Castle to London she had immediately planned many more.

"Trains! Trains" he had exclained at the time. "It is just a 'flash in the pan'. A few crashes, and everybody will be back riding horses or travelling in a wheeled carriage!"

Because his feelings had not changed it suddenly seemed ridiculous to be contemplating investing money in a Coal Mine.

Without really meaning to, he said aloud:

"I have a good mind to turn round and go home!"

Ilitta turned her face to look at him in astonishment.

"Why should you say that?" she asked.

"I have a feeling I am wasting my time, and I do not really want a Coal Mine!"

"Then you certainly must not buy one," she said.

"Personally I hate the idea of them, even while I realise that coal has become a necessity and something people cannot do without."

The Duke looked at her in surprise.

"You mean you have thought about coal before now?"

"Of course!" she replied. "I read the report on the horrors that took place in the past. Now the newspapers report that new safety devices have saved the lives of a great many miners, and the Davy Lamp has made all the difference to the men working below ground."

The Duke looked at her in astonishment.

"How do you know about such things?" he asked.

She laughed.

"I suppose you think I only read the fashion pages of magazines and the Court Circular in the daily newspapers!"

He thought a little ruefully that that was all the women with whom he spent so much time ever read.

Even when he made a powerful speech in the House of Lords and it was headlines in the newspapers they were unaware of it.

"Tell me why you are interested," he said thinking this was another unusual aspect of her he had not expected.

"Politics are about people," she said, "and people interest me even though I do think they look like animals!"

"I do not think our Statesmen would be particularly flattered!" the Duke remarked dryly.

"Of course I may be mistaken, because I have not seen many of them in the flesh," Ilitta said, "but at the same time from what I read in the Parliamentary Reports of their speeches they appear to me either like a lot of silly

62

sheep, or else turkey-cocks, puffed up with their own importance!"

The Duke laughed before he remarked:

"That is certainly very scathing!"

She glanced at him a little nervously as if she thought he was shocked by the way she had spoken.

But she saw he was smiling and his eyes were twinkling and she therefore said:

"When I get to London I will send you drawings of all the leading Politicians and you will be able to see whether I am right or wrong."

The Duke had the uncomfortable feeling that in quite a number of cases she would be right. But he replied:

"I hope that when our time together ends you will have given up this nonsensical idea of going to London alone."

She did not reply, but her eyes were on the road in front of her.

He knew without her saying so that he had not dissuaded her from her determination to go to London with or without his help.

A number of arguments came into his mind, then he thought it would be a mistake to bandy words at the moment, and better to concentrate on what lay ahead.

To change the subject he said:

"I think we ought to have some sort of arrangement by which you can tell me what you think of the gentlemen we are about to meet without their being aware of it."

"I have already thought of that," Ilitta said, "and if as you say we are meeting them for luncheon, I shall have plenty of time while they are eating to look at them, sense their vibrations, and know whether they are false or true, straight or crooked."

"Supposing you are wrong?" the Duke asked.

"That is a chance you will have to take," Ilitta replied. "After all when you engaged me you were betting on an outsider!"

The Duke laughed.

Because he was beginning to think there was no subject in which Ilitta was not interested he asked:

"I presume from that remark that you follow the racing reports."

"Of course I do," Ilitta replied. "Horses mean as much to me as I am sure they do to you, and I like to know which horses have won the major races, and why."

The Duke turned again to look at her before he asked:

"Are you telling me you have theories as to why certain horses win certain races?"

"Naturally!" Ilitta replied. "Although I am not often fortunate enough to see racing except in the part of the world in which I live, I follow everything that happens."

She paused to say in a more serious tone:

"It is not only breeding or form which makes a winner, but something a little extra, or different in a horse's training or in itself, that makes him win against other horses which seem his equal in every way."

Again the Duke was surpirsed, knowing this was something he had often thought himself.

It was what had made him convinced where his own horses were concerned that it was that little extra something which made them beat other equally fine specimens of horse-flesh.

Because it was a subject he found absorbing, they talked of nothing else all the last miles of the journey, and only ceased when Hanson interrupted them to say:

"We're just enterin' the village, Sir, and it'd be best when we gets there if we asks somebody where t'house is."

A few moments later they had turned into the long drive with a lodge on each side of the entrance gates which seemed to be in need of repair.

"I will let you know," Ilitta said, "some way or another what I think of these men, and please do not agree too quickly to what they suggest."

"Of course not!" the Duke answered. "This is only a preliminary visit, and I shall certainly send people of my

64

own choice to inspect the Mine and will read their report very carefully before I even consider buying it."

"I though you would say that," she said, "and of course it is very sensible of you!"

The Duke smiled a little mockingly, thinking it unusual that he should be commended for being sensible by such a young girl.

As the house they were seeking came in front of them, the Duke saw that it was a tall, square, rather ugly Georgian mansion built of grey stone.

He noted that the garden surrounding it was neglected and like the lodges the windows of the house needed painting and as he saw when they reached it, so did the front door.

Almost as soon as he drew up his horses beside a flight of stone steps Captain Daltry came hurrying down them, smiling at the Duke with delight at seeing him, and holding out his hand in welcome.

"You are exactly on time, Sir Ervan," he said, "in fact far sooner than I expected."

Then as he reached the Phaeton he looked questioningly at Ilitta sitting beside the Duke.

Hanson had already jumped down from the back and as the Duke stepped to the ground he took the reins from him.

Then without hurrying the Duke shook Captain Daltry by the hand and walked round to the other side of the Phaeton to help Ilitta.

As he lifted her down he thought she was as light as thistledown and nobody would suspect that she was a day over fifteen.

As they walked together round the vehicle to the steps he knew from the way she was moving beside him that she was enjoying the situation.

He thought it certainly made it more amusing for him to know that he had a private investigator of his own and that Captain Daltry was quite unaware of it.

"I have brought my sister with me, Daltry," he said.

"Let me introduce you: Captain Daltry – Miss Ilitta Trecarron!"

"I am delighted to see you," Captain Daltry exclaimed.

But as he shook her hand Ilitta was sure that was untrue, and he was in fact annoyed that the Duke was not alone.

"I have arranged," he said as they walked up the steps, "what I hope you will find an adequate meal, but with our host away enjoying himself in London, and most of the servants on holiday, it has not been as easy as I expected."

"My sister and I are quite used to roughing it," the Duke replied.

"I expect first you would both like a wash," Captain Daltry said. "I will take Miss Trecarron upstairs and she must, as I was not expecting her, excuse the rooms not being open or as well dusted as they should be."

He pointed out to the Duke that there was a cloakroom off the hall then walked ahead of Ilitta up a quite impressive staircase.

Although the walls were hung with many portraits, she noticed they were obviously by second-rate artists and were of dull and rather ugly people.

She supposed they were the ancestors of the owners of the house.

Captain Daltry hurried to open the door of a room leading off the landing on the First Floor.

The curtains were drawn and the wooden shutters were closed and he said as he crossed the room:

"Do not move until I have let in some light. I am afraid there will only be cold water on the washing-stand, but I will try to get some hot for you, although it may take some time."

It did not sound as though he was eager to do so and Ilitta said quickly:

"No, of course not! I can manage quite well with cold, and I have no wish to cause you any bother."

Captain Daltry having opened the wooden shutters to let in the light replied:

"It is no bother, and I am sure it is more pleasant for your brother to have you with him than if he were alone."

She had the feeling as he spoke that he was somehow deliberately making the best of a bad job.

She tried, because she wished to be fair, not to judge him too quickly, but to give herself time.

"I will be looking out for you when you come downstairs," Captain Daltry said, "but we are using a Sitting-Room that opens from the centre of the Hall, and you cannot miss it."

"Thank you," Ilitta replied.

He shut the door and she heard him running down the corridor, and wondered why he was in such a hurry.

Then she went to the washing-stand to find there was cold water in a china ewer as he said, but there was a layer of dust on top of it and she knew it had not been renewed for some time.

There was also dust on the floor and on the dressing-table and she thought that it was quite obvious there was no Lady in the house to supervise things.

She supposed in consequence that the servants in their master's absence had grown very slack.

She took off her bonnet, tidied her hair, retied the blue ribbons on either side of her head, and thought she looked a nice, simple school-girl.

But she was certain that Captain Daltry, intent on impressing his guest, would pay little if any attention to her.

This proved to be the truth, and as they sat at a large table in the Dining-Room Ilitta, listening to the four men talking, thought the whole arrangement was rather strange.

First of all there was no trained servant to wait on them but a man who from his appearance she suspected to be a groom in charge of Captain Daltry's horses.

He changed the plates awkwardly and made a lot of noise stacking them on a side-table.

Captain Daltry himself poured out the wine and his other guests passed the dishes that were arranged on a sideboard.

His friends were first to appear to Ilitta with animal heads almost as soon as she was introduced to them.

The one who Captain Daltry informed the Duke was his Solicitor was a small, beady-eyed, middle-aged man with pointed features.

The other was large, clumsy, and obviously badly educated.

They however did full justice to the food, piling it on their plates and eating with a greedy zest which seemed to suggest that they did not often enjoy such a lavish repast.

Captain Daltry had certainly made an effort, the Duke thought.

There was a whole salmon which he knew came from the Wye, there was a loin of pork, and a leg of lamb, and a brawn which had obviously been purchased from an Inn or a shop which specialised in the garnishing and presentation of such a dish.

Nothing, both the Duke and Ilitta knew, was home-cooked, though Captain Daltry had said:

"I hope you will find something to your liking. The Cook has done her best, but of course she is only a country-woman and not capable of providing elaborate dishes of the kind which I am sure, Sir Ervan, you enjoy at home."

As the Duke had the best French Chef in London and his cooks in the country were known as being experts in every type of cuisine, he merely smiled but made no comment.

To follow there was a Stilton cheese and a fresh loaf of bread which must have been baked within the last twenty-four hours.

What was good was the wine, and the Duke was aware as Captain Daltry kept filling his glass that he was determined to soften him up for what he was to see after luncheon.

He obviously was hoping to make him so muddle-headed that he would agree to any business terms he suggested.

He was, however, much too abstemious as a general rule and far too astute not to be aware of what was intended.

He soon realised that after every sip he took his glass was immediately refilled by Captain Daltry, that the claret was excellent, but definitely heavy, and not an advisable beverage for the middle of the day if one wanted to keep a clear head.

After the claret there was port and brandy at the end of the meal.

Because the Duke thought it was churlish to refuse both he asked for a very little brandy.

But he only sipped it, listening to his host who was going out of his way to be agreeable and amusing.

It was clear to the Duke that Captain Daltry was a past-master at being, as he would have described it, the 'life and soul of the party'.

The Duke noticed however that his Solicitor and the other large man made little or no contribution to the conversation.

Ilitta made no attempt to join in, and Captain Daltry ignored her as being unimportant.

All he wanted to do was to entertain the Duke, in fact the Duke had to admit to himself that Daltry was certainly trying 'very hard'.

It was however with a sense of relief that he was able to say:

"As time is getting on and my sister and I do not wish to be late in arriving at the house where we are staying the night, I think now we should go and inspect the Mine."

"Yes, of course," Captain Daltry agreed. "I think it would be easier, as it is somewhat difficult to find, if we travel in my carriages which are waiting outside, and your horses rest here until we return."

For a moment the Duke hesitated.

Then he thought that perhaps, as the journey this morning had taken longer than he intended, it would be good for his team to rest as much as possible, and he would tell

Hanson to be ready to leave as soon as they returned.

Accordingly, after Ilitta had run upstairs to get her bonnet and cloak, she found waiting outside the front door two closed carriages, each drawn by one horse.

They did not look very impressive, and she had the same idea as the Duke when he saw them, that they had been hired for the occasion.

The Duke and Captain Daltry were waiting for her by the leading carriage and she stepped in first. The Duke sat down beside her, and Captain Daltry on the opposite seat.

As the coachman drove off she handed the Duke a piece of paper on which she had written three words.

As she did so she said:

"These are the names of the horses about which we were talking this morning, and you asked me to write them down so that you could mention them to our host this evening."

"Oh, thank you!" the Duke said carelessly, understanding exactly what she was implying.

He looked down at the piece of paper which Ilitta had handed him and saw in very small writing, which could not possibly have been read from any distance, the three words she had written on it:

They were:

"Fox, Ferret, Baboon."

He read it carefully, then slipped the piece of paper into an inside pocket of his coat.

As they drove on he knew Ilitta had already made up her mind about the three men they had met and was telling him to be very much on his guard.

'Fox!' the Duke thought to himself. 'Wily, treacherous, untrustworthy, and might be dangerous!'

So that was how she saw Daltry!

He was not surprised and thought it was what he might have expected.

'Ferret' certainly described Daltry's Solicitor, and he

knew from the moment he had seen the man he would not have trusted him an inch.

'Baboon' was certainly very apt for the large, clumsy oafish man who had hardly opened his mouth at luncheon, except to put food into it.

It was difficult to imagine why Daltry considered it necessary for him to be there at what was supposed to be a business meeting.

However the Duke had no time for reflection because the minute they moved away from the house Captain Daltry started to talk about the Coal Mine.

He eulogised over its potentialities and the Duke thought he exaggerated almost ridiculously the amount of coal it was capable of producing in the immediate future.

"What is important," he finished by saying, "is that nobody here should have the slightest idea that you are contemplating buying the Mine. I have merely told some of the men who work in it that you wish to see how admirably they have managed to extract a very large amount of coal so far from the seam!"

He smiled before he added:

"But as you will have seen from the papers I sent you, they have only touched the 'tip of the icebeg', so to speak, and there are thousands and thousands of tons as yet unexcavated."

"I read your report thoroughly," the Duke replied.

"Then there is no point in going over it again," Captain Daltry said. "At the same time, I do want you to realise that this is the opportunity of a lifetime, something which may never come again."

He paused before he went on:

"Already the demand for coal has soared dramatically in the last two years, and with railways being planned from London to every large town in the country, coal is becoming as valuable as diamonds, although not so pretty!"

He laughed at his own joke.

As he did so the Duke noticed that his teeth were pointed and thought Ilitta was right.

He was undoubtedly like a fox, and just as untrustworthy.

Chapter Four

The village where the Coal Mine was situated was pictur-
esque and, Ilitta thought, surprisingly clean.

She had always believed, from what she had read, that
coal-mining villages were black from the coal dust and that
the people themselves gradually developed a dark skin
from continually either working in the mine or living on top
of it.

As the horses came to a standstill, Captain Daltry said to
the Duke:

"Do not forget you are just an ordinary visitor interested
in the countryside."

Ilitta thought he was rather over-emphasising what he
wanted them to believe and she was sure the Duke thought
so too.

They stepped out and walked some distance past a huge
slag heap to where some machinery rose high above ground
level, its wheels and iron girders being exactly what Ilitta
had expected to see.

There were a number of barrows to be seen, iron trolleys
in which coal was brought to the surface, and wooden
pit-props to support the roof of the shafts after the coal had
been extracted.

They drew nearer to the machinery and Ilitta noticed
some of it had been recently oiled, although she had the
idea there was underlying rust which had not been removed
first.

She wanted to point this out to the Duke but thought that
would be a mistake. Instead she followed him and Captain
Daltry into the mouth of the large cavern, in the centre of

which there was a shaft which led down, they were told, to the galleries from which the miners had already dug out coal.

There was a windlass which Captain Daltry explained was the normal means of letting the men down into the Mine and bringing them up again.

It looked a very primitive piece of apparatus and he said to the Duke in a low voice:

"Of course there is far more modern machinery in the larger and newer pits."

Then as if he was afraid someone might overhear what he said, he looked over his shoulder before smiling in a knowing manner at the Duke.

They stood looking at the windlass for a moment, and then the Duke said:

"Perhaps it would be a good idea if I went down to have a look. I suppose there are men working below?"

"Yes, of course," Captain Daltry said hastily, "but I think it would be a great mistake for them to see you. They would immediatly think 'something was up'."

This suggestion sounded quite reasonable and the Duke stared down into the pit, hearing nothing and seeing nothing but darkness.

Then he moved away through the outer cavern into the open air.

"What I want to point out to you now," Captain Daltry said, still in a low voice, "is the village itself. As you can see, the houses are in good repair, although some need a little paint, and the people look well and happy. I knew this would appeal to you, Sir Ervan."

"Of course," the Duke agreed.

Ilitta was certain he would want to talk to some of the villagers, who had by this time come to the doors of their cottages and were staring at the party with curiosity.

But Captain Daltry hurried them into the carriage and they drove back the way they had come.

"I did not really see all I wanted to," the Duke remarked.

"I could not allow you to get your clothes dirty!" Captain

Daltry replied with a smile. "And you have seen the reports of the engineers who have inspected the Mine professionally."

He smiled before he added:

"I can assure you that, as they stated very clearly, the seam is a very large one, and it will take at least twenty years before it is exhausted even if they do not find further seams branching off it."

He gave a little laugh, which to Ilitta sounded exactly like a fox's bark, before he added:

"In fact, it is a bargain which I cannot believe you would be so foolish as to miss."

The Duke did not reply, and while Captain Daltry chattered on he was silent until they were back at the house again.

Then as he stepped out of the carriage he said:

"Will you ask your man to order my Phaeton to come round immediately? My sister and I must be on our way."

"Of course," Captain Daltry replied, "but if you will come into the Drawing-Room where we were before luncheon, I would like a brief word with you before you leave."

The Duke could not refuse, but Ilitta thought he walked impatiently across the Hall and into the Drawing-Room.

She had supposed that Captain Daltry wanted to speak to him alone, but to her surprise she noticed that his Solicitor and the man she thought of as 'the Baboon' followed and stood just inside the door.

Captain Daltry crossed the room to a table on which there was an ink pot, pens and a number of papers. He looked down at them and then said:

"I would like your signature on this contract which will allow you to buy the mine, two villages, and 50 acres of ground for £10,000."

The Duke stiffened.

"You must be aware, Daltry, that I have no intention of immediately signing a contract, nor can I promise to buy the mine until my own people have investigated it fully."

"I have already told you that is quite unnecessary," Captain Daltry answered. "The reports I sent you are by men well known in the mining world."

"I, of course, take your word for that," the Duke replied, "but at the same time I never buy anything without first taking the advice of my own financial consultants."

Captain Daltry looked down at the papers on the table.

"There is no time for prevarication," he said. "The sum which is being asked for the Mine is so small that there must be a great number of other purchasers who will jump at the opportunity if you do not clinch the deal."

"I do not want to disappoint you after you have taken so much trouble," the Duke answered courteously, "but you did not make it clear to me before I came here that I was expected to make what one might call a 'snap decision'."

"That is what I require, and if you do not agree then the Mine may easily go to someone else."

"Then I must just wish them good luck," the Duke replied. "Now my sister and I really must be on our way."

He turned towards the door with his hat in his hand and as he did so, as if recognising a signal from Captain Daltry, the other two men stood immediately in front of it.

As the Duke said nothing but just stood looking at them, from behind him Captain Daltry said:

"Since you are being exceedingly foolish I must make the position a little clearer."

As he spoke he drew a pistol from his pocket and Ilitta gave a little cry of horror.

The Duke turned round slowly.

"Are you threatening me, Daltry?"

"What I am saying," Captain Daltry said in a very different voice from the ingratiating tone he had used since their arrival, "is that either you voluntarily sign this contract of sale or I shall use very much more stringent methods to make sure you do."

"Let me make myself understood," the Duke replied

loftily. "I have no intention of signing anything! I consider your behaviour disgarceful and I will make quite sure you are unable to behave like this another time!"

Captain Daltry laughed and it was a very unfriendly sound.

"I know exactly what is in your mind," he said. "You will see that I am barred from your Club and am no longer acceptable in what you consider Social Circles! Very well, I accept that, but my terms have now changed."

He paused as if he was waiting for the Duke to ask what they were, then as he did not speak he went on:

"I intended to enjoy myself with the £10,000 you were to pay for the Mine, and it is not a sum that you will miss with your large income…"

"I think this conversation is quite unnecessary," the Duke interrupted, "and I intend to leave immediatly."

He would have turned round, but Captain Daltry's pistol was pointing at him ominously.

"You will find it hard to do so," he threatened, "with a bullet in your leg and I am sure your sister is too young to be a very adequate nurse!"

Because he almost snarled the word, Ilitta instinctively moved a little nearer to the Duke as if to beg him to be cautious.

The Duke was aware as she did so that her presence considerably lessened his chances of escape.

He thought he could have managed somehow to disarm Daltry without getting injured, but while he did not think the man Ilitta described as a 'Ferret' would be much trouble, he was less sure about the 'Baboon'.

As if he knew what he was thinking, Captain Daltry said:

"I am not speaking idly when I say I will shoot you to prevent your leaving here. Moreover I would like you to know that my friend Albert here was the champion wrestler of Lambeth, and I think even someone with your athletic record would find him a difficult opponent to overcome."

He was sneering, and Ilitta felt that now he was more like a wolf than a fox and very frightening.

She moved closer still to the Duke as Captain Daltry went on:

"You have threatened to take your revenge on me if I compel you to hand over the £10,000 we first discussed. You will therefore now pay double that figure for your freedom, as it will entail my having to go abroad."

His lips curled mockingly as he continued:

"I am sure you would not wish me to be anything but comfortable in France, or anywhere else I am obliged to settle, until you have forgotten that you suffered at my hands the first failure of your life!"

Again he was sneering unpleasantly, and his pointed teeth seemed even more prominent as he did so.

"You have stated your terms," the Duke said. "I must naturally ask for time to consider what I can do about it and discuss it with my sister."

"That I will grant you," Captain Daltry replied, "and you will not be surprised to know that I had already thought that might be your attitude!"

He did not lower the pistol as he went on:

"Had you been alone I intended to put you downstairs in the cellar and keep you there until the damp and the rats spoke more eloquently than I am able to do."

He looked away at Ilitta before he went on:

"Of course being a humane man I could not subject anything so young and pretty to such deprivation. You will therefore be imprisoned, and I am sure that is a word you understand, in the attic."

He paused impressively, before he continued:

"Perhaps a cold night and the fact that even after such an excellent luncheon you will soon be hungry, will help you to realise on consideration, that £20,000 is quite a small payment to ensure you will not only be free but uninjured."

The way he spoke was so frightening that hardly

realising what she was doing, Ilitta slipped her hand into the Duke's and felt his fingers close over it.

Then as he still did not speak Captain Daltry continued:

"My friends will escort you upstairs, but as you go remember I am behind with this pistol pointed at your back and my finger on the trigger!"

Ilitta knew by the vibrations she felt coming from the Duke that he was furiously angry but at the same time uncertain what he could do.

She realised as he had, that without her he might have pitted his strength against all three of the men and trusted to his expertise in the boxing-ring and his exceptional physical fitness to effect his escape.

Yet if they did knock him unconscious or, as Captain Daltry had threatened, shoot him in the leg or in the back, she would be left defenceless and a weapon in their hands which they would undoubtedly use.

The Duke drew in his breath and then said calmly:

"I will give you my answer to your proposition when I have had time to consider it."

He turned as he spoke and walked towards the door still holding Ilitta by the hand.

The Solicitor hurried ahead of them, Albert kept by their side and Captain Daltry walked behind, his pistol pointing at the Duke's back.

They went up the staircase to the first floor, up another flight of stairs to the second, and again up a steep flight which led to the third.

Here the passage was narrow with a number of doors opening out of it, and Ilitta knew they were the servants' quarters.

The floor was covered in dust and they passed half a dozen doors before reaching one which was open. She felt that one of the men, perhaps Captain Daltry himself, had come upstairs to inspect it while they were washing before luncheon.

The room which they entered was certainly bare and

cold. An attic bedroom with an iron bedstead against one wall having only a mattress on it and no other bedding.

The chest of drawers had several of the handles missing. There was a wash-basin with a cracked ewer and a chipped china bowl, and in front of the small empty grate there was a tattered rag rug such as Ilitta knew the cottagers made to sell for a few pence.

"As you can see," Captain Daltry said sarcastically, "there is every comfort, and for your pretty sister there is an almost identical room which opens out of it."

Bowing his head under the sloping ceiling he led the way into another room which was even more unprepossessing than the first.

Here another iron bedstead was tied together with string, but there were two threadbare blankets lying on the worn mattress and on the wall above the bed a text embroidered with coloured wool.

There was no rug on the floor, while the chest of drawers had a broken leg and was propped up on a brick.

After a quick glance round, Captain Daltry returned to the first room from which the Duke had not moved, although Ilitta had followed him.

"If you are thinking of escaping," he said, "let me tell you that Albert will be on guard in the passage outside and I shall be downstairs ready to shoot anyone who in the darkness I might so easily mistake for a burglar."

He walked to the door but looked back to say:

"If you are not ready to sign by the morning I feel quite certain your sister will persuade you to be sensible. Starvation is invariably a very compelling argument."

He walked from the room without waiting for a reply and shut the door. They heard first the key turn in the lock and a heavy bolt put in place and then the same treatment to the room allotted to Ilitta.

As they heard footsteps moving away down the passage, Ilitta threw herself against the Duke and cried:

"Do they mean it? Do they really mean to leave us here

to starve if you do not give them the money?"

The Duke automatically put his arm around her. He did not look at her but stared with unseeing eyes across the room.

"There must be some way we can get out of this mess," he said in a low voice.

As he spoke so calmly, she knew he was determined if it was humanly possible not to surrender.

She felt her fear slip away from her and she smiled.

"As we obviously cannot leave by the 'door," she said in a whisper, "what about the window?"

They moved together to the window to find it was a very small casement under pointed gables which Ilitta remembered now she had noticed at the very top of the house.

She could also remember, and one glance confirmed it, that there was a sheer drop to the ground and to escape that way one would need to have wings.

There was no need to say anything as each knew what the other was thinking, and moving from his arm which was around her shoulders Ilitta sat down on the bed.

As she did so, she found the matress was extremely hard and probably stuffed with straw.

"What are we to do?" she asked.

"I admit it is difficult to think of a plan," the Duke answered in such a low voice she could hardly hear him.

"I knew they were unpleasant, crooked and wily," she said, "but not as bad as this."

As she spoke she opened a small handbag, attached to her wrist by ribbons, in which she carried her money.

In it was the pencil with which she had written down for the Duke what animal she thought each of the three men was like, when she had first seen them.

Now with the pencil in her hand she jumped up from the bed and going to the wall started drawing.

It was a white-washed wall and she managed with a technique which the Duke much admired to depict

Captain Daltry with a fox's head which made it still easier to identify him.

The Ferret was smaller but it was a recognisable portrait and then towering over them both, large, clumsy and somewhat menacing, was the wrestler with a Baboon's head.

It took her a very little while to draw them, and as she did so the Duke, sitting on the bed watching her, thought no other woman he had ever met could behave so well in what he was well aware were very unpleasant circumstances.

He was quite sure that Captain Daltry would keep to his threat and imprison them in the attic until they agreed to his terms.

Too late he realised he had played into the man's hands by agreeing to his condition of secrecy and telling no one, not even his mother, where he was going.

The Marquess of Buxworth would have no inkling except that he had not turned up as expected, and Lord Armitage who was expecting him this evening would be disappointed.

"What can I do?" he asked himself.

He looked round the room desperately, as if he expected some other exit would reveal itself besides the locked door and the window with an eighty-foot drop beneath it.

Then as Ilitta put the finishing touches to her caricatures of their jailers the Duke walked restlessly through the open door into the next bedroom.

Because he was so tall he had to bend his head and shoulders to pass beneath the sloping roof.

But once inside the room he felt it was hardly worth the trouble. It was just as secure a prison as the one next door.

Then as he was about to return to Ilitta an idea came to him and he looked up at the ceiling.

It was not at all far above his head and was stained with damp, especially near the window, where the plaster was peeling away from the wall.

As he looked more closely he saw what he was seeking,

and as he stared upwards Ilitta came in from the next room.

"I wondered what you were doing."

The Duke put his fingers to his lips to ensure her silence and then he pointed to where just above the window there was a square to be seen on the ceiling which he knew was a trap-door leading up to the roof.

It was something which was to be found in attics of most old houses and was the only means by which workmen could reach the roof to repair it when rain came through the tiles or tiles themselves were blown away in a gale.

As Ilitta looked up the Duke fetched a hard chair from the other side of the room and climbing onto it started to press the flat of his hand against the trap-door.

At first he did so tentatively as if to test how firm it was, and then more forcefully as he realised it would have been painted over the last time the room was decorated which was obviously a long time ago.

It took a great deal of strength before suddenly with a bang the trap gave way beneath his pressure and fell backwards with a crash.

Quickly the Duke got down from the chair, and covering his mouth with his hand so that his voice sounded as if it came from a distance he said:

"What is the matter? Have you hurt yourself?"

He looked at Ilitta as he spoke and she understood that someone might be listening to what they were doing.

"No, it is all right," she cried, raising her voice as if she were in the next room. "I only knocked over a chair. I think its leg is broken."

"Better the chair than you," the Duke replied and Ilitta managed a little laugh.

Then he took her by the hand and drew her back into the next bedroom.

They sat down side by side on the bed and he said:

"I think we may be able to escape by the roof but it is important to investigate before it gets dark. I rather doubt whether our host will allow us candles in case we set the house on fire."

Ilitta nodded and then said:

"I will do the investigating. You must stay here in case they speak to you."

She saw the Duke was about to argue and said:

"If he does come back, you can say I am asleep and that you do not want to disturb me. But if you do not reply he will be suspicious and may come in to investigate. They might even put us in the . . cellar."

There was a little tremor in her voice and the Duke knew that like most women she would be afraid of rats.

"Do you really think you can explore the roof?" he asked.

"I am sure I can," Ilitta said. "We have the same sort of gables at home, and I have often climbed over the rafters when exploring or playing hide-and-seek."

She could see that he was not quite convinced and she added:

"You must admit I am lighter than you, and it is very easy to slip and come through a ceiling."

"Very well," the Duke agreed, "but you must promise me you will not do anything dangerous. You must just find out if there is any possible way of escape. Then come back and tell me what you have discovered."

Because she knew it was a mistake to talk more than necessary, Ilitta merely nodded and getting up went into the next room.

First she took off her bonnet and her cloak and laid them down on the bed.

Then she covered them with the blankets hoping that at a casual glance anyone would think she was lying down asleep.

To make it more realistic she took off her slippers and arranged them so that they stuck out, looking like two feet, from under the blanket.

She knew as she did so that the Duke's eyes were

84

twinkling as if he appreciated how clever she was being. Then she went and stood beneath the open trap-door and looked at him.

He picked her up by her knees and lifted her gently until she could climb through the opening onto the rafters.

As she expected, there was quite a lot of light, not only from several small skylights of glass that had been inserted obviously to help any work that had to be done on the roof, but also because there were several slates that had either slipped or been blown away.

Slowly, because she knew it would be a mistake to hurry, Ilitta crawled from one joist to another.

She was very careful not to slip between them and, as she had told the Duke, put her feet through the ceiling of one of the rooms.

Not that she was sure there was anyone in them, but the fall of plaster might make a noise and alert the Baboon if he was listening.

It seemed a very long way to the end of that part of the house and her knees were beginning to ache and so were her shoulders from crouching down beneath the sloping roof.

Finally she saw a blank wall ahead of her and for a moment was afraid that there would be no way out except through one of the rooms.

Then as she reached the very end of the attic and was thinking she must turn back she saw first a light coming from beneath her and then with a leap of her heart the top of a workman's ladder protruding from a small opening.

Resting on one of the joists was a hammer and a screwdriver as if someone had been working on it recently.

Ilitta looked at the ladder which led down to the passage on which their bedrooms were situated and where the Baboon, Albert, was supposed to be acting as sentinal.

Then she could see by craning her head backwards there were doors not only on the side of the passage where their rooms were situated, but also opposite.

She was certain these led to cupboards or small bed-rooms which in many large houses had no outside window, but where the lowest and least important kitchen-maid or housemaid slept until they were promoted to larger and better bedrooms.

Her mother had always refused to use them in her home because she thought they were unhealthy.

Nevertheless they were there as part of the architect's design, and Ilitta was certain now that if the Baboon was on duty he would have make himself as comfortable as possible by sitting or lying in a room opposite the door he had to watch.

Anyway there was nothing she could do but take a chance on it, although she had the feeling the Duke would expect her to go straight back to him.

'I must find out a little more,' she thought, and turning round felt with her stockinged feet for the first rungs of the ladder.

A moment later she was in the passage and saw as she expected a staircase, very much the same as that up which they had come, which descended just inside the end wall of the house and she suspected led to the kitchens.

She began to creep down it, listening all the time for the sound of anyone moving or speaking, being sure that in such a large, empty house sound would travel a long way and she would have time to hide before she was seen.

She reached the second floor and seeing that the stair-case descended again she thought this would be the way for them to escape.

Then suddenly she heard someone cough in a room on her left-hand side.

She stood very still, every muscle in her body tense, and wondered whether she should try to run back the way she had come or look for somewhere to hide.

When the cough came again she knew it was made by a very old person and therefore not one of their jailers.

It was then, almost as if she was being directed, that what

she called her perception told her that the person coughing was someone she could trust and who would help her.

The sound had come from the first room in the passage next to the staircase and she went to the door, knocked on it gently and when there was no answer, opened it.

She saw she was in a fairly large bedroom and seated in an armchair in front of the fire was an elderly man.

He had white hair and she saw at a glance he was somewhat frail. He had an old woollen shawl around his shoulders and was holding out his hands towards the fire.

Quietly she shut the door behind her and walking towards him said:

"Good-evening. I heard you coughing and wondered if I could help you."

The old man looked up, peering at her with bleary eyes, one of which was beginning to develop a cataract.

::Who be ye?" he asked. "Yer b'aint one o' them gentlemen who said the Master'd told them they could take over the house for a day or so."

"No, I am not," Ilitta answered, "but you must tell me who you are."

"I be in charge 'ere," the old man said. "When the Master – Mister John as I always calls 'im havin' known 'im since he were a boy – was goin' off with his Regiment, he says to I 'you and your wife look after the house until I come home. I know I can trust ye.' "

Ilitta sat down on a wicker-seated chair which was near the old man's. As she was cold she, too, put out her hands towards the fire.

"You say your Master is with his Regiment," she said remembering Captain Daltry had said he was amusing himself in London.

"Aye, he be away in some outlandish place," the old man said. "But'll be 'ome soon. I 'ad a letter from 'im two weeks ago, saying 'e'd be back by Christmas."

"That is good," Ilitta said. "Did you already know

these friends of his who said he had told them they could use the house?"

"Never set eyes on 'em," the old man replied. "They gives I five shillings to get out of the way, sayin' they wanted th' kitchen and everything else for themselves."

He lowered his voice as he looked towards the door.

"Yer won't tell 'em that I'm still in the 'ouse? They tells I to go to th' village."

"No, of course I will not tell them," Ilitta said. "And if you would like to hear the truth I do not believe your Master told them they could come here and do as they liked."

The old man tried to sit up in his chair.

"What be ye sayin', Missie? Are ye tellin, me they be burglars?"

"No, they are not burglars," Ilitta replied, "just crooks, and they are trying to sell a gentleman the Coal Mine."

"Sell th' Coal Mine?"

The old man stared at her in astonishment, then started to laugh which made him choke and cough for some minutes.

"Can I get you some water?" Ilitta asked.

"Nay, it's all right," he managed to say, "but ye made me laugh!"

"Because I said they were selling the Coal Mine?"

"There b'aint more than a bag o' coal to sell."

"Are you sure of that?" Ilitta asked.

" 'Course I'm sure. Th'old master, Mister John's father, closed it down six year ago."

"Because the coal had run out?"

"That's what I told 'im. I were the overseer in charge of the Mine."

Ilitta drew in her breath.

"You tell me there is no coal there?"

"A lump or two for anyone who wants to dig it for their own grate, but most of 'em prefers wood."

"You were the overseer, so of course you know."

" 'Course I do. There were plenty of coal when I first comes here and it lasted for about ten year. Then it come to an end. The Master were very generous. He offered the men work on th' land and only a few refused and went off to Wales. There be plenty o' coal there."

Ilitta was fascinated to receive this information, and kept her eyes fixed on the old man who seemed glad to have someone to talk to.

"I be glad not to be workin' at 'em Mines now I be so old," he went on. "I've bin happy here since Mister John asked me an' me wife to come and look after th' house for 'im."

"Where is your wife now?"

"She died three months ago," the old man said. "and lonely I be without 'er."

"I can understand that," Ilitta said. "It must be very sad for you."

" 'Er were a Cornish girl, from Cornwall like meself."

Ilitta smiled.

"I wondered what your accent was."

"Accent, is that what ye calls it. Though I s'pose all Cornish people speaks alike."

"That's true," she said, "and so do we in Worcestershire."

"That be so," the old man agreed.

"Do you miss Cornwall?" Ilitta asked.

"Aye, but I 'ad to come away," the old man said. "There be plenty of copper in the Mine there, as I tells 'Is Grace, but he shut it, sayin' 'e did not like to think of any human being spendin' 'is life in th' dark."

"Was it a Duke you were working for?" Ilitta asked.

"Aye, indeed, the Duke of Marazion. A fine gentleman, an' very understandin' he was and could not bear to see a man or beast sufferin' if 'e could 'elp it."

The old man paused and gave a little cough before he went on:

"That were why 'e closed down th' Mine though I tells him he was shutting away a fortune."

He gave a laugh before he added:

"But Dukes be so rich they don't need money like ordinary folk."

Because of the way he said it Ilitta laughed too, and then she said:

"Well, I rather sympathise with your Duke in saying that human beings should not always be in the dark. But now I must go back the way I came before it gets too dark for me to find the way."

Ilitta got to her feet and the old man said:

"Ye be a pretty girl and I like talking to ye. Come and see me again."

"I might do that in an hour or so," Ilitta replied. "Would you mind?"

"I'd say welcome to ye. Then I can tell ye more about the old days."

Then a little apprehensively he said:

"Yer'll not say to 'em people downstairs I be 'ere?"

"No, I promise you," Ilitta said, "and if by chance they find you, please do not say you have seen me."

"I'll not breathe that I've seen a sign nor sight of ye," the old man said, then laughed and brought on another fit of coughing.

"You keep warm," Ilitta said. "I promise you I will come back later."

She took one of his hands in hers and felt how thin and frail it was.

"It has been very nice meeting you," she said softly.

"Thank ye, dear. Thank ye," the old man replied.

She slipped away, opened the door and shut it very quietly and crept back up the stairs.

She prayed as she reached the top floor, but since now it was getting dusk she was certain that even if Albert was looking she would seem in the distance nothing but a shadow.

Quickly she climbed back into the roof and hurried over the joists.

It was much darker than it had been before, but she did

not falter and when finally she looked down through the open trap-door that led to the bedroom she saw the Duke looking up at her.

She could see by the expression on his face that he had been anxious during her absence.

But now she had returned he put up his arms and laying her hands on his shoulders he skilfully but gently lifted her down.

Then for a moment he held her close against him and she felt that it was like coming home to safety and that the strength of him made her feel secure.

When she looked up into his face she thought there was a strange expression in his eyes, but because she was so excited at what she had to tell him she said in a whisper:

"It is all right! I have found a way by which we can escape and I have so much to tell you!"

Then, with what she thought was almost an abrupt movement the Duke took his arms from around her and said:

"That is what I am waiting to hear."

Chapter Five

Sitting beside the Duke on the hard mattress Ilitta told him excitedly what she had discovered and how she was certain the old man could tell them how to get out of the house without being seen.

She knew he was delighted at her news.

At the same time he was very careful to keep his voice low, as she realised, to make it sound as if they were depressed and worried about the situation in which they found themselves.

As she finished she asked:

"Shall we go now? At once?"

The Duke shook his head.

"I think that would be a mistake. Since it is now nearly dark it would be exceedingly difficult not only to make our way along the attic without a light, but also to find our way through the rest of the house."

Ilitta knew he was being sensible, but she gave a sigh before she said:

"I am so anxious to escape."

"So am I," the Duke replied. "At the same time we have to plan every move we make and not make a mistake."

She knew he was thinking of how ruthless Captain Daltry might be if he thought his prisoners were trying to escape and would not hesitate to put into action his threat to shoot the Duke in the leg.

"What I am going to suggest," the Duke said, "is that we rest until dawn, when it will be just light enough to see our way out."

She smiled at him and realised as she did so that since she

had returned the room had grown very much darker.

It was not only dusk outside, but she thought she could see the glimmer of the first evening star.

"I have another suggestion to make," the Duke said quietly.

"What is that?"

"When I am travelling in a very cold climate, I and the men with me are all sensible enough at night to lie close to our horses. That is often essential, unless one wants to wake up in the morning and find oneself turned into an icicle!"

Ilitta prevented herself from laughing, but she gave a little chuckle.

"Although it may seem slightly unconventional," the Duke went on, "I propose, since we have no horses with us, we lie close together, otherwise I am afraid you will find yourself very stiff in the morning."

Ilitta did not hesitate.

"Of course I see that would be the sensible thing to do," she said, "and which of the rooms in our magnificent Suite do you suggest we use?"

"I have made some investigations while you were gone," he replied, "and I found there is one tattered bolster which will do for our heads and, believe it or not, another blanket!"

"That is certainly an unexpected luxury," Ilitta teased.

The Duke rose from the bed which was in her room and as he did so picked up her cape which was still lying behind him on the mattress.

She saw that he had already removed the blankets and found he had placed them on the bed next door.

By now it was difficult to see, but she was aware that he was taking off his coat and she knew that he had already removed his boots before her return.

He lay down on the bed, then put out his arm and she knew he expected her to put her head against his shoulder.

She felt as she did so that the closeness of him was not

93

only warm and comforting but also gave her a feeling of security.

As soon as they were lying together the Duke first wrapped one of the three blankets over their feet, then arranged the other two to cover them both, and finally Ilitt'a lined cape on top.

As he lay back Ilitta was aware how wise he had been.

Now that the excitement she had felt at coming back to him was over, she realised it had grown very cold, for the attic was not only extremely chilly but also damp.

Then as she moved instinctively a little nearer to the Duke she could feel his heart beating and thought it was quite extraordinary to be in the arms of a man she had met only yesterday.

Yet she felt as if she had known him all her life and he was somebody she could trust implicitly.

She was not even quite certain what she meant by the word 'trust'.

She just knew she could rely on him and that because he was there she was not really afraid.

In fact, the terror she had felt when she entered his bedroom to escape from the man breaking into hers had almost been forgotten.

"Go to sleep," she heard the Duke say, "I will wake you when it is time for us to make our escape."

"We must on no account over-sleep."

"I will not do that," he answered. "I have grown used, on my travels, to waking at whatever time is necessary."

"I would like you to tell me about your travels."

"I think you would find them quite interesting," the Duke replied, "but now I want you to rest."

It made Ilitta happy to know he was thinking of her.

She knew he would protect her, and once again she was thinking of him as a Royal standing on top of the moors with his horns silhouetted against the sky.

"I am very lucky to have found him," she told herself, and without realising it snuggled a little closer.

The Duke however was awake, watching through the window one by one the stars coming out in the sky.

He was puzzled with himself over the strange sensations he had felt when he saw Ilitta looking down at him through the trap-door in the ceiling.

He had been worrying because she had been so long, and hoping she had not had an accident or perhaps been caught by one of their jailers.

Then he told himself that if that had happened she would have shouted for him as she would have, had she got into difficulties in the attic.

To keep himself occupied he had searched in all the drawers of the chests in both their rooms and found, as he had told her, the bolster and the extra blanket.

He was well aware how cold their attic bedrooms would become during the night, and thinking how the servants in big houses were often badly provided for he was determined that should not happen in any of his.

He wished there was some way he could light a fire.

It would be easy to break up the chairs and even the drawers in the chests, but it was only wishful thinking, and once again he was back to wondering why Ilitta was taking so long.

Only when he was growing really worried did he look up and see her smiling down at him.

Her fair hair, falling forward, framed her face and he knew by the sparkle of her eyes she was bringing him good news.

He put up his arms eagerly.

Then as he lifted her down, finding it easy because she was so light, he held her for a moment against his chest and found that the blood was throbbing in his temples!

Suddenly he had an almost irrepressible desire to kiss her.

She looked so lovely as she stared up at him, her eyes wide and shining, her lips parted in her eagerness to tell him what she had found, that it was only by a superhuman effort of self-control that the Duke did not hold her lips captive with his.

Then he knew not only would it frighten her, but it would be very wrong of him to destroy her trust in him.

Instead, he forced himself to sit down on the bed beside her without touching her, and concentrate on what she was saying.

But he knew that with every breath he drew he wanted her in a strange way that was quite different from the burning desire he had felt for many other women.

Then inevitably there had been a joint need for each other which had made two fires flare up, leaping higher and higher until they became one.

But with Ilitta it was completely different.

Now as he held her in his arms he was aware by her soft breathing and the stillness of her body that she was drifting into sleep.

As he felt his heart beating with an irrepressible desire, at the same time he knew he wanted to protect her and keep her from anything that might harm or frighten her.

He was aware of the same sweet scent coming from her hair that he noticed when he went to her room at the Inn and he tried to put a name to it, but failed.

Then as more stars filled the sky he though that what his mother had prayed for had come true and he had found the perfect woman who had always eluded him.

Not, as he suggested laughingly, on the top of the Himalayas, nor at the source of some unexplored river, or outside the Acropolis in Athens.

He had found her in a servants' attic, cold, cheerless and damp, where they were both the prisoners of an unscrupulous man who was demanding a ridiculously large sum of money in ransom.

The Duke thought, as he drew Ilitta a little closer to him although she was unaware of it, that he would give half his fortune to save her from suffering or from being frightened.

At the same time, everything that was adventurous and courageous in him fought against having to give in tamely to what he admitted to himself was a very clever piece of roguery.

The Duke could commend Daltry for at least being original in thinking of selling a Mine in the absence of its owner and even commandeering his house to make the whole deal seem more plausible.

He knew from what Ilitta had discovered that Newall himself had no part in this game.

But it had been sharp of Daltry to create a situation in which, if he had been complacent, he would have accepted the reports, paid for the Mine, and found he had lost £10,000 without anything to show for it.

The Duke was quite certain that Daltry had gambled on the assumption that he would not like to be made to look a fool and would therefore not have sued him for obtaining money by false pretences.

It would be very easy to prove Daltry guilty.

At the same time, if he had been so foolish as to trust the crook, to expose it would have damaged his reputation for always being a winner, both on the Race-Course and in the athletics in which he participated.

"It will teach me a lesson," the Duke told himself. "At the same time, although Daltry will not be aware of it, fate in the shape of a fog has brought me something so valuable, so precious, that it is worth a million times more than any Coal Mine in the whole country!"

He thought how thrilled his mother would be when he told her about Ilitta.

Then with a faint smile he remembered he knew nothing whatever about her: who her parents were, where she came from, and whether from his family's point of view she would be considered worthy of being his wife.

But he told himself that if she came from the gutter it would not matter; if she was the daughter of a coal-miner he would still want to marry her.

However, he knew for certain that every movement she made and every word she said proclaimed her to be of gentle birth and undoubtedly his equal, however undistinguished her family tree might be to his.

He kissed her hair and felt it soft and silky against his lips.

"I love you, my darling!" he said in his heart. "And when we are free I will tell you so."

It seemed very strange to him that this was the first time he had held a woman in his arms who had not been acutely conscious of him as a man, while at the same time he was very much aware that she was a woman.

But by now Ilitta was sleeping deeply and contentedly as a child might have done.

The Duke thought it was one of the most fascinating experiences he had ever known to find somebody so completely unselfconscious, innocent, and unspoilt in a world that was full of women who used their feminity as a weapon to ensnare and entice every man they met.

"I love you, my precious!" he said in his head.

Then he wanted the night to pass quickly so that he could talk to her and see the little dimple on the side of her mouth when she smiled at him.

*   *   *

Ilitta felt herself coming back through wave upon wave of sleep as the Duke moved very slowly and gently.

It took her a second to realise where she was and what had happened.

By now the Duke had left her and she opened her eyes to see in the first faint light of the dawn that he was standing beside the bed.

She did not speak because she remembered immediately how important it was that they should move silently.

Quickly she threw off the blankets and walked on tip-toe in her stockinged feet into the next room.

The Duke followed her and she bent down only to pick up her slippers which were lying on the floor.

98

She held them in her hands, and the Duke having followed her with his coat and her cape over his arm laid them down on the bed.

Then putting his hands round her knees as he had done yesterday, he lifted her up into the opening over their heads.

When she was inside the attic, Ilitta paused for a moment to make quite certain she was moving the easiest and quickest way to the end of the building, knowing the Duke would be following her.

Then she was aware he was handing something up to her and bending down took it from him, to find it was his boots.

She put them carefully on one the joists, then moved away to leave him plenty of room to lift himself lithely up by his hands until he was crouching down beside her.

She smiled at him, but they did not speak.

Then Ilitta set off slightly encumbered because she was carrying her slippers.

She realised that while the Duke had put on his smart grey whipcord driving-jacket, he still had to carry his boots and her cape, although they did not appear to incommode him.

Once again there was a long way to crawl over the slats beneath the roof.

Because there was still very little light she had to watch every movement so as not to slip.

Then at last she reached the end of the house and knew there was always the chance of their being seen as they descended the ladder and moved across the passage in which the Baboon was supposed to be watching for them.

She was sure the Duke had been wise in waiting until this hour by which time sleep would have overcome the wrestler and he was doubtless snoring peacefully, not contemplating for a moment that they could get away.

At any rate there was no sign that he had heard them as they hurried down the next flight of stairs.

Without knocking Ilitta opened the door into the room where she had talked to the old man.

She was not surprised to see the fire burning in the grate and instead of being in bed he was still in the armchair, wrapped in his shawl with a rug over his legs which were resting on the seat of another chair.

There was a candle beside him although it had burnt low and as soon as she came into the room he opened his eyes.

"Ah! It be ye again!" he remarked.

"Yes, I have come back," Ilitta said, "and I have brought with me a friend who is escaping, as I am, from those men who have no right to be in your Master's house."

"I'll see Mister John deals wi' they when 'e come back!" the old man said.

"What is more to the point," the Duke said in his quiet voice, "we want you to tell us how to get out of this house without anybody seeing us."

"Where be ye a-goin'?" the old man enquired.

"To the stables," the Duke replied. "My horses are there. Then this young lady and I can ride away before they try to stop us."

"Be ye careful!" the old man worried. "I don' know what Mister John'll say, 'avin' people like they usin' 'is house, an' sellin' 'is Coal Mine wot ain't got no coal in it!"

He looked at Ilitta as he spoke and gave a little laugh which turned as usual into a cough.

"We must hurry," the Duke said, "so will you please tell us how we can reach the stables."

"Go down the stairs . . ." the old man began.

He then described quite clearly the way they must go until they came to a door which led into the garden.

"No one'll see ye there," he added, "if ye keep in they bushes, an' stables be to t'right o' ye."

"Thank you very much," the Duke said, "and when your Master returns I will write and tell him how well you have looked after us."

"That be right kind o' ye, Sir. I would'n' want 'im

thinkin' as I'd failed in my duty, lettin' they crooks in when 'e were away."

"You could not have stopped them," the Duke said, "so just keep out of sight until they have gone."

He put two sovereigns into the old man's hand and while he was staring at them incredulously Ilitta bent forward to cover his hands with hers and said:

"Thank you . . thank you very much! I am sure your wife wherever she is, is thinking of you and still loving you."

She saw the tears come into the old man's eyes.

Then before he could reply, she and the Duke had slipped out of the room, shutting the door very quietly behind them.

Hand in hand they went down the next flight of stairs and followed the old man's directions, until just as he had told them they found a door that led into the garden.

The Duke drew back the bolts taking great care to make no noise.

Then the cold air was on their faces as they moved quickly through the shrubs until just in front of them they saw the opening into the stable-yard.

Now they paused and Ilitta's fingers tightened on the Duke's because she was afraid Captain Daltry's groom would be up and hanging about and would see them.

The Duke moved ahead, entering the stable by the first door he came to.

There was a long row of stalls and Ilitta, with a leap of her heart, saw the Duke's team and only one other horse which was obviously not well bred and rather rough, which she supposed belonged to Captain Daltry.

To her surprise the Duke was looking in all the empty stalls until he stopped and opened one of them.

As he did so she saw Hanson sleeping on a pile of hay.

The Duke moved to his side and putting a hand over his mouth before he woke him asked in a whisper:

"Where is Daltry's groom?"

"He be up in th' attic, Sir," Hanson replied. "I stayed 'ere to be near t'horses."

"Quite right!" the Duke approved. "Now we have to get away quickly and the best thing to do is to ride."

Hanson started to his feet and as the Duke gave his instructions Ilitta was sure that he had been in a tight corner with his Master before.

He was obviously not surprised at anything which happened, but was ready to adjust himself to any circumstances however unexpected.

The Duke certainly wasted no time.

They found saddles hanging on the walls, and by a piece of good fortune there was a lady's saddle which was placed on the back of one of the Duke's horses for Ilitta.

She understood without being told that they would all ride, leaving the Phaeton behind which could be collected later. She and the Duke would each ride a horse, Hanson riding the third and leading the fourth.

All the time they were bridling, saddling, and tightening girths on the horses they were listening to hear if there was any movement from the groom overhead.

"He 'ad a lot of ale afore he went t'bed," Hanson whispered. "It'll tak 'im some time to sleep it orf!"

He grinned as if he enjoyed outwitting the man who Ilitta thought had doubtless been told to keep an eye on him.

When the horse the Duke was saddling was ready, he went out to explore how they should leave the stable.

On one side the yard was not far from the house and led directly onto the drive.

To ride that way would mean they could be seen from any window, and again without the Duke saying anything, Ilitta thought he was afraid that Captain Daltry might, if he saw his prey escaping, fire at them.

Instead, the Duke discovered at the back of the stable there was a door leading into a paddock.

He pointed it out to Hanson to show him that was the better way to go.

Moving as quietly as they could, the Duke went ahead leading his horse, followed by Ilitta with Hanson bringing up the rear with the last two of the team.

Outside in the paddock the Duke lifted Ilitta into the saddle, and only as she smiled down at him when he had done so did she realise she had not brought her bonnet with her.

She wondered if he thought she looked very untidy with her hair flowing over her shoulders.

Actually, he was thinking that she looked so lovely, with the first rays of dawn rising up the sky behind her, that she might have been the 'Spirit of the Morning'.

Then he told himself severely that the quicker they were away the safer they would be, and swinging into the saddle led the way across the paddock.

He saw a gate at the far end and thought he should open it for Ilitta.

As if she knew that was he intended she pushed her horse ahead and leapt over the two-barred fence that surrounded the paddock with a grace that made him smile as he hurriedly followed her.

Hanson, however, with two horses to control was more cautious, and when Ilitta and the Duke looked back they saw him quite a long way behind them, but by now they were all out of sight of the house.

It was then that Ilitta spoke for the first time since they had left the old man.

"We have done it!"

"I know," the Duke agreed, "and I have never felt so delighted since I won the Gold Cup at Ascot!"

She laughed and he continued:

"I only wish I could see Daltrys' face when they open our bedrooms to see if cold and hunger have had the effect he expected and find us gone!"

"It was clever of you to find the trap-door."

"And very clever of you to find that nice old man who told us the way out," the Duke replied.

103

"You will not forget to write to his Master as you said you would?"

"You are insulting me! I always keep my word!"

"Of course! I would not expect anything else."

They smiled at each other.

Then as the sun rose they were galloping over the fields with an elation that they felt not only because they had triumphed over the enemy, but also because they were together.

They had gone several miles when the Duke said:

"I think my host might be surprised to see me so early in the day, and as I am in fact extremely hungry, I suggest we stop somewhere for breakfast."

Since they were in what appeared to Ilitta to be an uninhabited part of the country, she asked:

"How do you suggest we do that, unless, as you suggested before, we eat grass?"

"I have a far better idea than that," the Duke said. "I am going to find a Farm House and beg them to be hospitable to three very hungry travellers."

"It sounds to me as if that is something you have done before!"

"Not always in this country," the Duke replied, "but Arabs are very generous to strangers and Monasteries in Tibet never turn anyone away."

Ilitta gave a little cry of delight.

"Now you are beginning to tell me about your travels," she said, "and that is something you promised me you would do."

"At the moment I would rather talk about food," the Duke said, "or better still—eat it!"

He spurred his horse as he spoke and they galloped on until in about half a mile they saw in front of them an attractive black and white Farm House.

Black and white buildings were relics of Tudor times and were characteristic both of Worcestershire and Gloucestershire. The Duke thought as he approached the Farm that it looked prosperous and he was sure it would be a very hard-hearted farmer's wife who would not refuse his request for breakfast.

*　　*　　*

A little later the Duke and Ilitta were seated in a comfortable Parlour with a fire blazing away in the grate.

As the farmer's daughter, a buxom young woman, was laying on the table a cottage loaf of newly baked bread, a huge pat of Jersey butter and a comb of honey, Ilitta said with a little laugh:

"If you tell anybody what has happened to us since breakfast yesterday they will not believe you!"

"That is why we must be careful what we do say," the Duke replied.

She looked at him quickly before she asked:

"Are you going to keep it a secret?"

"I am just considering what would be best."

He was sitting back in an armchair with a skilfully crocheted anti-macassar behind his head, while Ilitta having discarded her cloak was seated on the fur hearth-rug enjoying the warmth of the fire on her face.

She looked at him for a moment before she said:

"I may be wrong, but I have a feeling you will not wish your friends to know how you were deceived and threatened by a man like Daltry."

"That is the truth," the Duke agreed. "It is the sort of story that would go round the Clubs like wild-fire and be exaggerated and contorted out of all proportion. And of course, they will make the most of the fact that I was accompanied by a very beautiful young woman!"

"But you made it quite clear that I was your 'sister'."

"Of course," the Duke answered, "but in a way that makes it worse, since I should never have allowed my sister to have become involved with a man like Daltry."

"But he thought I was a child."

"You are not as young as all that," the Duke replied,

"and being a responsible brother I am very particular about whom my sister meets."

Ilitta thought over what he had said before she asked:

"What story will you tell Lord Armitage?"

"I think it would be best to say that we were held up not only by the fog, but also because we had a slight accident with the Phaeton," the Duke answered after a moment. "We therefore were forced to leave it behind and ride the horses."

Ilitta clapped her hands.

"That is very clever of you!"

"Fog is always unpredictable at this time of the year," he went on, "and it is, in fact, very easy to have an accident when caught in one."

"And where will you tell them we stayed last night?"

"At the place where I first met you," the Duke replied. "We just forget the very unpleasant episode at Mr. Newall's house, and as doubtless Lord Armitage will have heard of him, or may even know him, it would be a mistake for us to embroil him in this particular drama."

"You had better tell your man Hanson what you have decided."

"Of course," the Duke said, "and as I just now heard him coming into the yard with the horses I will go and speak to him and see that he has some breakfast."

He went from the room and Ilitta looked into the fire thinking what fun it all was.

'How could I have known . . how could I have guessed,' she thought, 'that so many exciting things would happen to me in the space of a few hours?'

At the same time she remembered how frightened she had been when the man had approached her in the Coaching-Inn, and had then broken down the latch of her door.

'There cannot be many men like that in the world,' she thought to herself. 'How very, very lucky I was that Sir Ervan was there!'

As she thought of him her eyes softened.

She had never imagined a man could be so handsome in a way she could not explain, so authoritative and competent and at the same time so gentle and considerate.

She was not tired because she had slept so peacefully in his arms.

Now she thought it seemed shocking and reprehensible to have spent the night so close to a man who was, in fact, a stranger.

But it was, as he had said at the time, the sensible thing to do.

If she had been in the stables she would certainly have snuggled up to her horse for warmth.

The Duke came back into the room and she felt her heart give a leap because he looked so attractive and was smiling at her.

"You have told Hanson?" she asked.

"I have told him!" the Duke replied sitting down again in the armchair.

"He will make no mistakes when we arrive at Lord Armitage's house?"

The Duke shook his head.

"Hanson has been with me for many years, and although I have not taken him on my more extensive travels abroad he had always been prepared, as he says himself, for emergencies, and actually enjoys one."

The Duke did not add that he had said to Hanson outside in the yard:

"And do not forget, Hanson, that the young lady with me is my sister, Lady Georgina. It would be a great mistake for His Lordship to think she is anyone else."

There was a knowing look in Hanson's eyes which the Duke thought was slightly impertinent, but there was nothing he could do about it.

He added:

"Inform the servants in the brake that we met Lady

Georgina in the fog and she also had to take shelter at the Inn."

He did not wait for Hanson to reply but walked away, eager to return to Ilitta.

As he did so he thought that no woman he had ever known could look so beautiful first thing in the morning, and at the same time be completely unconcerned about her looks.

It also amused him how, when the farmer's daughter came in with a huge plate of eggs, ham and sausages, Ilitta's face lit up with delight as she exclaimed how hungry she was.

It had become fashionable amongst the sophisticated women with whom the Duke spent so much of his time, to be very careful what they ate in case it should increase the circumference of their tiny waists.

He was used to see them picking at their food and while they looked wistfully at the exotic dishes his Chef had provided, permitted themselves to enjoy only a mouthful or two.

Ilitta, while she looked, the Duke thought, like a nymph who had just emerged from the mist, managed to eat two eggs, several sausages and three slices of ham.

She had then munched a crust of warm bread having spread it thickly with butter and honey.

"I do not think I have ever enjoyed a meal more!" she exclaimed.

"I must commend you," the Duke replied, "for not complaining."

"What about?"

"The discomforts of last night and the fact that our jailers did not allow us even a drop of cold water to drink."

Ilitta gave a little chuckle before she said:

"Do you think they would really have kept us locked up until we were starved into submission?"

"I am quite certain of it! Daltry must have spent a lot of money, which I imagine he can ill afford, on the luncheon

108

he provided us with yesterday, the set-up outside the Mine, the carriages which took us there, and of course the travelling expenses for himself and his companions from London."

"No wonder he will be furious when he finds us gone!" Ilitta exclaimed.

"You can draw me a picture of their discomfort," the Duke said, "and I am sure Daltry will severely punish the Baboon for letting us slip through his fingers."

Ilitta had a vision of the wrestler's huge hands and the bulging muscles of his arms and shuddered.

"We will forget about it," the Duke said. "Except that it will be a wonderful story one day to tell our children and our grandchildren."

"Of course!" Ilitta exclaimed. "I will make it into a book and illustrate it for them!"

The Duke knew as he spoke that he had been thinking of children of his of whom Ilitta was the mother, but it had never crossed her mind that there was anything personal in his remark.

They did not hurry over their breakfast and only when Ilitta exclaimed that she could not eat another mouthful did the Duke say reluctantly:

"I suppose we ought to be on our way."

She looked at him, then she said:

"Perhaps now . . as you no longer have any need of my services . . I should . . leave you."

It was a question which the Duke thought he should have expected, and he replied hastily:

"No, I cannot allow you to do that. Besides, as you have been so helpful and saved me from such an ignominious situation, I feel so responsible for you that if you still wish to go to London, I will take you there."

She stared at him for a moment, incredulous. Then she asked:

"Do you really . . mean that?"

"Of course," he said. "I can hardly allow you to travel on

a Stage Coach and risk being accosted by some other swine of a man, as you were the night we met, or worse still encounter Captain Daltry and his friends also returning to London."

He thought as he spoke, the latter was a rather clever point to make.

Ilitta gave a little cry.

"I never thought of that! Of course it would be a great mistake to go to London at the moment, unless I was with you."

"I tell you what we will do," the Duke said. "We will stay the night with Lord Armitage. I know he has never seen my sister and will therefore accept our story exactly as we tell it. Then tomorrow we will make plans if you wish to go to London, or stay with another friend of mine."

He thought as he spoke that by the time they left Lord Armitage, he would have been able to tell Ilitta how much he loved her, and learn what her response would be.

But looking at her he knew she had not the slightest idea what his feelings for her were, and she was in fact treating him exactly as if he were her brother.

It was a somewhat sobering thought that for the first time in his life the Duke found himself questioning a woman's feelings for him.

Always before, he had known by the sparkle of desire in their eyes, the provocative twist to their lips, and the way in which their hands instinctively went out towards him, that they were his for the asking.

But Ilitta treated him as she had from the very first, as somebody she could trust who would protect her and save her from being frightened, but otherwise was as impersonal as if he really were her brother, or even her father.

"I have to make her love me," the Duke thought.

He knew that even if it was as difficult as climbing Mount Everest or diving down to the depths of the Atlantic it was something he must ultimately achieve.

In the meantime he was aware because she was so young

that he would have to approach her very carefully.

He had always thought to himself that one could not anticipate or demand trust. It was something two people gave each other and it came from the heart.

But if it was once abused or damaged, it was impossible to repair.

"She trusts me," the Duke said to himself, "and I swear I will never fail her!"

The sun came though the window and turned Ilitta's hair to gold, and he thought with it flowing on each side of her face and over her shoulders she looked so young that it seemed almost wrong and unnatural that he should want her as a woman and as his wife.

And yet he had known when she lay close to him last night that she excited him wildly.

At the same time he had a respect and reverence for her because she was different, because, as his mother would have thought, she had belonged to him through millions of years and would be his for all eternity.

He knew that before he claimed her he had to awaken her to the realisation of what love between a man and a woman meant.

It would be the most thrilling and exciting thing he had ever done in his life, although it would doubtless prove the most difficult.

He was thinking so deeply of Ilitta that it was quite a surprise when she asked:

"You are quite certain you really . . *want* me to come with you? I would not want to be an encumbrance. After all, as you know, I did force myself upon you."

"Very much to my advantage," the Duke replied. "If you had not been there and told me very clearly that Daltry and his friends were crooks, I might have been stupid enough to – agree to his 'proposition' as he called it."

"Fox! Ferret! Baboon!" Ilitta recited. "I am glad that I was not mistaken in seeing them as they really were!"

"Well one good thing is that they will not trouble us

again," the Duke said. "I can only hope that our host tonight will not turn out to be a man-eating Tiger!"

"I think that is unlikely," Ilitta laughed, "but if he is, I will certainly warn you."

They lingered a little longer in the Farm House and talking to Ilitta made the Duke laugh in a whole-hearted way that was different from the sophisticated laughter with which in the past he had greeted the innuendos that were so much part of his conversations with women in London.

After Ilitta had tidied herself and washed her hands, she came downstairs to find the farmer's daughter red-faced with delight at the generous manner in which the Duke had paid for their breakfast.

The horses were waiting for them outside and they set off with Hanson behind them, not hurrying but enjoying the Autumn sunshine and talking on all sorts of different topics.

The Duke told Ilitta of a journey across a desert and how once he had got lost in a sandstorm.

He related too the story of a long trek to the Caucasus, finding its mountains, forests and gorges very different from any other part of the world.

"You are so lucky," she sighed. "You have done so many things I have longed to do, and met people I have only read about in books."

"There is plenty of time," the Duke said, "and perhaps your husband, when you have one, will take you to all the places in the world you want to see."

To his surprise Ilitta stiffened and said sharply:

"I have no wish to be married!"

"Why not?" the Duke asked.

"For reasons of my own, and I do not want to talk about it!"

She made her horse, as she spoke, go faster and it took a minute or two for the Duke to catch up with her.

Then he said:

"I am interested. Tell me why you do not wish to get married. All women should be married."

"That is a man's point of view!"

"And most women's" the Duke replied speaking from experience.

"I want to study painting and be myself."

"Alone?"

She did not answer and he saw the colour come into her face and knew she was thinking of the dangers of being alone.

He had the feeling, although she had not said anything, that she was not as keen on going to London as she had been, and certainly for the moment did not wish to leave him.

It was a start in the right direction, he thought, but he was not certain what the next step should be and he told himself he must proceed very slowly and not rush his fences.

Because the Duke had broken in many young horses he was aware that they had to be handled with care, kindness, forethought and most of all, with understanding!

The same, he thought, might apply to Ilitta, and while he was prepared to give her all those things he also knew that every moment they were together his love for her was increasing.

He could hardly believe what he was feeling, knowing it was so unlike his usual approach to a woman de desired but infinitely more exciting and more marvellous.

His mother had told him that for her love had come at first sight.

That was not literally true in his case, except that he thought now that when she came into the room and he had known that he must help her and protect her it was love, although he had not recognised it.

There could be no doubt, however, that what he now felt was a love that he had never known before, except in his dreams.

When he had seen Ilitta looking down at him through the trap-door he had thought she was an angel peeping through the clouds.

'I love her!' he almost said aloud, as he looked at her riding beside him, with her golden hair flowing over her shoulders.

She was exquisitely graceful, and because she was happy, the sun seemed to have been caught in her eyes and was not only on her face, but coming from it.

Because they had lingered on the way it was getting on for luncheon time, which the Duke thought was a respectable hour at which to arrive, when they saw Lord Armitage's house ahead of them.

It was a fine example of Georgian architecture and impressive so that Ilitta was immediately conscious of how inadequately dressed she was and with nothing to change into.

As if once again the Duke was reading her thoughts, he said:

"Do not worry! Armitage is a widower, and I do not suppose he will have a big party for me."

"Perhaps you can think of a reasonable excuse as to why I have no luggage," Ilitta suggested. "Your brake should be there by this time, so you will have plenty of fresh clothes."

The Duke thought for a moment. Then he said:

"I could say that you were travelling with me for only part of the journey and your luggage had gone ahead to where you were to stay with friends. When we were caught in the fog we of course stayed together in the only place we could find shelter."

Ilitta gave a little cry.

"You are wonderful! You can think up plausible explanations for everything, and of course that is a very credible story. Then I can look pathetic and borrow from somebody, if there is anybody to borrow from."

"I am sure there will be. I cannot remember, as I have never stayed with Armitage before, but I think he has some daughters and one of them should be about your age."

"I can only keep my fingers crossed," Ilitta smiled.

As she spoke she was hoping she could borrow some clothes in which she would look attractive for the Duke.

She was very conscious that the gown she was wearing and in which she had crawled about in the attics looked very much the worse for wear.

'Perhaps he will not notice,' she thought. 'At the same time, because he is so handsome himself, I want to look as if I really was his sister.'

They rode up to the house where grooms appeared as if they had been waiting form them, and two footmen came down the steps from the front door.

Then as they reached the hall a jovial, middle-aged man appeared.

"Welcome, my dear Duke!" he exclaimed. "I am delighted to see you!"

Only as Lord Armitage spoke did the Duke remember that, although they had talked about so many things, including the story they were going to tell, he had not revealed to Ilitta his real identity.

He had in fact completely forgotten about it until this moment when Lord Armitage addressed him by his correct title.

It was too late to do anything about it now, and having shaken his host by the hand and seeing him glance enquiringly at Ilitta he could only say:

"I am sorry I was unable to let you know in advance, but owing to the fog which upset all my plans and those of my sister, Georgina, I have been obliged to bring her here with me."

"And I am delighted you should do so." Lord Armitage said. "How do you do, Lady Georgina! It is a great pleasure to meet you!"

The Duke was aware that Ilitta had given a little gasp when Lord Armitage had addressed him as 'Duke', but with a control he admired she dropped His Lordship a graceful curtsy before she replied in a voice that had only a slight tremor in it:

"Thank you . . very much for . . having me!"

"I was taking my sister to stay with friends of hers," the Duke said, "but owing to the fog we were obliged to stay the night in a most uncomfortable Posting-Inn."

He smiled before he added:

"You will hardly believe it, Armitage, but I had a slight accident with my Phaeton and therefore had to leave it behind."

"I do not believe it!" Lord Armitage exclaimed. "As the champion driver who has won every contest in Britain, how could you, of all people, have an accident?"

"I can only blame the fog," the Duke replied.

"I heard it was very bad North of here," Lord Armitage admitted.

"It was, and because of it my sister's luggage is mislaid as it went ahead of her to where she is to stay."

"Do not worry, do not worry!" Lord Armitage said. "My daughters can provide whatever is required. One of them who is about the same size is unfortunately away at the moment, but Harriet is here and looking forward to meeting you."

Taking command of the situation, Lord Armitage sent the Butler upstairs to hand Ilitta over to the Housekeeper, then took the Duke into the Drawing-Room where his daughter Harriet was waiting for them.

As if the Duke had not had enough surprises for one day, Harriet was certainly something he had not expected.

Lord Armitage's elder daughter, who was married to the *Comte de* Soisson and lived in Paris, was on a visit to her father.

She looked like an exotic orchid and seemed very out of place in an English country house.

116

Having been married when she was eighteen, nine years in France had given her all the poise, sophistication, and allure of the French which the Duke had found very fascinating in the past.

But now, with his new feelings for Ilitta, he merely thought the *Comtesse* was overdoing the very obvious manner by which she set out to attract him.

He thought with a twinkle in his eyes that he knew every move she would make, almost every word she would utter, and could anticipate all the innuendos she mouthed so beguilingly.

He told himself he was far more interested in talking about horses with his host, but in actual fact he was waiting for Ilitta to come down the stairs.

He hoped she was not overawed or embarrassed by the grandeur of the house and the number of servants that appeared to be everywhere.

Footmen with powdered hair and a very elaborate livery brought in the champagne.

The Duke had noticed there were six of them waiting in the hall, and he had a feeling that Ilitta would find the Housekeeper in rustling black silk, a silver chatelaine at her waist, somewhat awe-inspiring.

It was the sort of thing taht had never troubled him before, but now he worried because she was away for so long before she came into the room.

When she did so he realised she had taken advantage of Lord Armitage's promise that she could borrow anything she required and was wearing a very attractive gown.

Of pale blue it was a perfect frame for her golden hair, clear white skin and large eyes.

Her hair still fell over her shoulders, but now the ribbons had been changed to match her gown and as she walked towards the Duke he felt as if she radiated a special light that came from the Celestial Spheres.

"I see we have managed to fit you up, Lady Georgina," Lord Armitage remarked.

"Yes, thank you. I am very grateful. My brother and I had to ride, although I did not even have a riding-habit with me!"

"I am sure our troubles are now over," the Duke said reassuringly.

He thought as he spoke that Ilitta would turn to smile at him and they would share a secret that no one else in the room would understand.

But to his surprise she did not look at him, and he felt sure it was because she had learnt he was a Duke and was perhaps either annoyed or shy because he had deceived her.

Then Lord Armitage was introducing her as the Duke's sister and he was aware that the *Comtesse* with an almost perfunctory nod was bored by the idea of a school-girl being in the party.

"I have heard so much about you, Duke," she was saying in a soft voice that was like the cooing of a dove.

"I hope it was to my advantage."

"Of course, even in France you are a hero, especially after you beat their champion swordsman."

"That was some years ago!"

"But they still talk about it, just as they talk about *you*," the *Comtesse* said.

She set out to flatter him and to make sure that he spoke to no one else all through luncheon.

"Not knowing what time you would be arriving and taking into consideration you were coming," Lord Armitage said, "I arranged a party for tonight, as quite a number of people are anxious to meet you."

He gave a short, abrupt laugh before he added:

"Need I add that they are all keen race-goers, and I imagine the conversation will be about horses, horses and more horses!"

It was what the Duke had expected when he had asked if he could stay with Lord Armitage, but now a soft voice in his ear said:

"Not if I can help it! There are so many more interesting things I can tell you about!"

The Duke thought a little cynically that he knew them all, had heard them all, and the *Comtesse* would be merely a repetition of what he had sampled before and always found disappointing.

But while he made some obvious remark he was glancing across the table at Ilitta, wondering what she thought of the *Comtesse*, and wishing he could be alone with her.

When luncheon was over they moved out of the Dining-Room to make inevitably for the stables.

Ilitta went with them but the *Comtesse* made some excuse to stay in the house.

The Duke was sure it was because horses bored her, although she must have ridden before she was married.

Ilitta, he thought, was as eager as he was to see Lord Armitage's extremely fine horses, many of which he had bred himself.

At the same time, as they went from stall to stall and were shown breeding mares and their foals, all of which took a long time, the Duke knew there was a barrier between himself and Ilitta which had not been there before and which made him very apprehensive.

He was aware that she never once looked at him and, although she answered when he spoke directly to her, the closeness there had been when they had breakfast together had vanished.

By the time they returned to the house the Duke had the despairing feeling that Ilitta was slipping away from him and he was losing her.

Then he told himself he was being imaginative.

After all, tomorrow they would be alone together, and he was quite certain that he would be able to explain away his change of name and persuade her it made no difference what he was called.

Also that as a man he was somebody very important in her life.

Chapter Six

The Duke planned that he would try to get Ilitta to himself after tea.

It was the usual elaborate meal in the Drawing-Room with a multitude of cakes, sandwiches and hot scones, and the *Comtesse* looking very elegant as she poured from a silver teapot.

As they talked around the table the Duke kept glancing towards Ilitta, feeling that if he could 'catch her eye' she would understand that he wished to speak to her alone.

But she was obviously determined to remain aloof from him, and he felt that to announce deliberately that he wanted to speak to his sister might cause comment.

The *Comtesse* made it very clear that she wished to talk to him, and as they both new Paris well and had a number of mutual friends in London it was not difficult for her to monopolise the conversation.

The Duke however managed to say to Lord Armitage:

"One thing I must do before I leave is to send a note to the Marquess of Buxworth apologising for my non-appearance, although I suspect he will guess that it was the fog which prevented me from reaching him."

"Buxworth will certainly be dissapointed not to have seen you," Lord Armitage replied, "and you would have enjoyed his horses. He has two superlative stallions which I would like to own myself, and several breeding mares which are exceptional!"

"I am sorry to have missed them," the Duke said, "but unfortunately my sister and I must leave tomorrow as we have to hurry south."

He thought this might tell Ilitta that he would be only too agreeable to take her to London if that was what she wished.

But still there was no response and Lord Armitage said:

"If you wish I will arrange for a groom to take your letter to Buxworth. Across country he is only about seven miles from here, although it is double, or nearly treble by road."

"That is very kind of you," the Duke said, having hoped that this was what his host would say.

He therefore rose to his feet saying:

"I would like to write the note now, if that is convenient."

"Of course," Lord Armitage agreed. "There is a desk in my Study where you will find everything you require."

The Duke looked at Ilitta.

"I think you ought to come with me and add your apologies to mine."

She rose reluctantly, he thought, then she came to his side and they followed Lord Armitage from the room.

He led them across the hall into a large Study where most of the wallspace was covered in books but which also displayed two very fine pictures by George Stubbs.

The Duke expressed admiration for them and Lord Armitage went into a long description of how he had bought one of them very cheap, as its owner had no idea of its value, while the other was a painting of his great-grandfather's horse which had won the Derby.

The Duke while appearing to be interested was thinking not of the pictures but of Ilitta, who was looking at the books and, he thought, had almost forgotten his existance.

At last Lord Armitage left them alone saying:

"I will order the groom to take the note as soon as you have it ready. If he sets off at once he will be back before it is dark."

"Thank you very much," the Duke replied automatically. "I am sorry if it is a bother."

"No bother at all, my dear Duke!" Lord Armitage said

in his genial manner. "I am only too delighted that the fog did not prevent you from staying here tonight."

He shut the door behind him and the Duke looked at Ilitta who had her back to him and said:

"I am tempted to use a hackneyed expression: 'At last we are alone!' It is certainly hard for me to speak to you in this house."

She did not reply but put the book she was holding in her hand back on the shelf, and walked across the room towards him.

There was an expression on her face he did not understand but he said quickly:

"Do not be worried! Everything is perfectly all right. We will leave early tomorrow morning, and go wherever you wish."

She parted her lips as if to speak, but before she could do so the Study door opened and the *Comtesse* came into the room.

"You are taking a long time to write one small note," she said, "unless of course, it contains expressions of love!"

She moved with a sinuous grace towards the desk adding:

"I have something very important to show you in the Picture Gallery, and it is a pity to waste any more time."

"I am not wasting my time," the Duke replied, "and because your father has been with me I have not yet written my note to Buxworth."

He sat down at the desk as he spoke and picking up the pen said:

"I will come to the Drawing-Room later, *Comtesse*, and then you can show me the pictures you have in mind. But for the moment I must be polite and do my duty."

The Duke thought he had made it quite clear that he did not want her presence, but she merely gave a provocative little laugh and said:

" 'Duty' is such a dull word! I will show you how to write a letter of love!"

It was the sort of thing the Duke was used to hearing, but not in front of Ilitta.

As he expected, she had moved away from the desk as soon as the *Comtesse* came to his side and he thought she would return to her perusal of the books.

Instead of which, swiftly, so that it took him by surprise, she reached the door, opened it and even as he called out: "Stop, Ilitta! I want your help!" had closed it behind her.

Having written the note while listening to the *Comtesse*'s blandishments as he did so the Duke left the study to find the Marquess.

He reached the hall and found the Butler was waiting to take the note from him saying as he did so:

"The groom's outside, Your Grace."

As the *Comtesse* was beside him there was nothing the Duke could do but follow her into the Drawing-Room where he found to his consternation on entering it, there was no sign of Ilitta.

He had the idea that she would have gone to her bedroom, but it was impossible to follow her without being rude to the *Comtesse*, until it was time to change for dinner.

As he went up to dress he told himself it had been a terrible mistake to bring Ilitta here, and if he had had any sense he would have taken her immediatly to stay with his mother.

At the same time he had not foreseen that his real name would have had such an effect on her, or that the pleasure that she had obviously felt at being in his company, even if it was nothing more personal, should disappear so quickly.

His own valet who had come with the brake was now looking after him and because he was thinking about Ilitta he said:

"Hanson told you, I know, that the young lady with me is, as far as His Lordship and anyone else in the household is concerned, my sister, and there must be no suspicions that it is not the truth."

" 'Course not, Your Grace," the valet replied, "an' we've all carried out Your Grace's orders an' nothin's bin said except what a pretty young lady she is!"

The Duke gave a sigh of relief.

He blamed himself for being so foolhardy as to bring Ilitta here.

Although Lord Armitage was unlikely ever to meet his real sister, there might be all sorts of repercussions he had not anticipated.

"The sooner we can get away the better!" he told himself.

Then he wondered how he could reassure Ilitta that once they were on their own everything would be all right.

There was a knock on the door and his valet going to open it had a conversation with the footman outside.

Then he came back to say:

"I've bin asked to tell Your Grace that Lady Georgina's got a 'eadache and asks if you'll make Her Ladyship's excuses as she'll not be dining downstairs this evening."

"A headache?" the Duke exclaimed.

He was determined to talk to Ilitta and find out what was upsetting her.

After all, he told himself, there was no reason why he should not go to his sister's room.

He finished dressing, thinking irritably that the *Comtesse* would make the very most of having him to herself.

He also had the uncomfortable suspicion that when the guests had left she would expect a great deal more than he wished to give her.

"I have a good mind to leave after dinner!" he muttered.

Then he knew it was impossible to take his horses out on a dark night when there was no moon, in a strange part of the country where he did not know the way.

He was therefore feeling unusually frustrated as he walked along the passage which led to the main stairs.

He had sent his valet ahead of him to find the maid who was looking after Ilitta, and as he reached the landing he saw an elderly woman in a white apron and starched cap coming towards him.

"I understand, Your Grace, that you wishes to speak to Her Ladyship."

"Yes, I do!" the Duke replied firmly.

"Her Ladyship's havin' a bath at the moment, Your Grace, and she says perhaps you could come and say goodnight to her later."

She was not a very perceptive woman, but she was nevertheless surprised at the way in which the Duke's eyes seemed to light up, and the manner in which he smiled before he said:

"Tell Her Ladyship I will do that."

He went downstairs thinking that everything would be all right once he could talk to Ilitta alone.

For the first time it struck him that the reason why she was not coming downstairs to dinner was that as she obviously lived in this part of the world, she was afraid one of Lord Armitage's guests might recognise her.

It was something he should have thought of himself, and it passed through his mind that ever since he found he was in love he had been behaving very foolishly.

He was actually, although it seemed incredible, forgetting his usual efficiency which ensured that he never made a mistake.

The dinner-party was exactly what he had expected.

The majority of the guests were men who spent their lives on Race-Courses, and while they might own very fine and well-bred horses appeared inevitably to have somewhat dull wives.

The *Comtesse* sparkled like a diamond amongst them and, the Duke thought, she was just as hard as that precious stone.

She was certainly witty and the men eyed her either roguishly or warily, and the women with dislike.

She made it quite clear however where her interest lay.

Sitting next to the Duke at dinner she made every effort

125

to prevent him from talking to anybody else, and tried to keep him away from the subject of horses.

She partially succeeded and the Duke who was beginning to find her tiresome had his revenge later by keeping the gentlemen in the Dining-Room talking of racing for over an hour-and-a-half after the ladies had withdrawn.

He was pleased to find that because some of the guests had quite a long distance to drive before they reached home most of them wanted to leave early, and the party broke up before midnight.

Even so, it seemed to the Duke that the hours passed very slowly before he could see Ilitta.

Never in his whole life could he remember being so anxious to be with a woman who was not equally eager to see him.

Before he could go upstairs however he still had to contend with the *Comtesse*.

As Lord Armitage went into the hall to say goodbye to the last of his guests the Duke and the *Comtesse* were alone in the Drawing-Room.

She came nearer to him and said in a low, seductive voice:

"It has been impossible to talk to you tonight with all these people here as I wished to do. My room is just across the passage from yours."

The desire in her slanting eyes and the manner in which her red lips curved over the words made it impossible for him not to understand what she wanted.

It struck him that in the past this was exactly what he would have expected to happen and what he would have been churlish to refuse.

But all he could see was Ilitta's child-like innocent eyes looking up into his and the dimple at the side of her mouth that had never been kissed.

He knew too, that the heavy, exotic French perfume the *Comtesse* was using made him long for the spring-like

126

fragrance of Ilitta's hair that he had kissed last night without her being aware of it.

Even to think of the softness of her body against his made him want her with such an overwhelming desire that he was astonished at the violence of it.

Never in all his numerous love-affairs had he felt as he felt now for a young girl to whom he meant nothing but somebody trustworthy and protective.

He was spared from having to reply to the *Comtesse*'s invitation as her father came back into the Drawing-Room.

"I hope you have enjoyed the evening, Duke," he said, "and now may I give you a 'night-cap'?"

The Duke however refused, and as Lord Armitage poured one for himself he explained:

"As it happens, I was extremely uncomfortable last night on a very hard mattress, and I am very tired. But let me thank you for a very pleasant evening before I fall asleep."

He smiled as if he had said something amusing, then raised the *Comtesse*'s hand to his lips.

"Goodnight, *Comtesse*!" he said. "Perhaps we shall meet again in London when I am not so fatigued."

Then he turned away, but not before he had seen the expression of anger and frustration in her slanting eyes.

He crossed the hall and went up the stairs quickly, determined to say goodnight to Ilitta, but hoping that the *Comtesse*, at any rate, would not be aware of it.

He knew she thought of Ilitta as being his school-girl sister and of no consequence.

At the same time, the Duke had learnt from long experience that women could be very perceptive about each other.

As the *Comtesse* was at this moment doubtless extremely annoyed with him, he did not want her to avenge herself on Ilitta, however young she might appear to be.

127

He reached her door, knocked gently and turned the handle.

As he expected she was in bed, and there was a lighted candle beside it.

He walked across the room and saw as he reached her that she was asleep.

She was sleeping as she had last night, on her side, but now her cheek was against the white linen pillow and her golden hair fell over it and over her shoulders outside the sheets.

It was a large bed with curtains hanging from a gold corolla and the Duke thought she looked very frail and insubstantial, not like the Spirit of Spring which he had thought her to be earlier this morning, but more like the Princess in a Fairy-Tale.

He stood looking down at her, wondering what she would feel if he woke her with a kiss.

Then he told himself that she was sleeping because she had been through a very exhausting experience and it had undoubtedly taken its toll.

There had been first her fear of the man in the Inn which had brought her to him for protection, and then Captain Daltry's behaviour which would have terrified most women into fits of hysterics.

Their escape had been highly dramatic, but in spite of the nervous strain she had played her part with a calmness and intelligence which had astounded him.

Looking down at her now it seemed extraordinary that anyone so young and inexperienced could have taken what had happened 'in her stride'.

She had neither complained, screamed nor fainted as he was quite certain any other woman of his acquaintance would have done.

"She is unique!" he told himself, and longed to wake her up and tell her so.

Then for the first time in his life the Duke put his own desires aside and thought selflessly of somebody he loved.

'Let her sleep,' he thought. 'There is always tomorrow, and thank God, we shall be alone!'

He bent down and very gently, so as not to disturb her, he kissed her hair as he had done last night without her being aware of it.

Again there was that scent of flowers to which he could not put a name.

Then he stood looking at her, thanking God he had found her and knowing that she was everything that would fit into his life as if they had been made for each other which he believed they had.

"You are mine!" he said in his heart. "Mine, and I will love you and adore you for the rest of my life."

He blew out the candle and groping his way across the room shut the door very quietly behind him.

* * *

The Duke lay awake for a long time thinking of Ilitta and how lucky he had been to have found her.

How could he have imagined, he asked himself, that a fog could change his life so completely that he felt he was no longer himself but some stranger whom he had to get to know through Ilitta's eyes rather than his own.

When he did sleep he dreamed a strange dream in which he was pursuing her over roof-tops and down Coal Mines but always unable to catch up with her.

He was just thinking despairingly that she was riding a horse that was too fast for the one on which he was following, when he was awoken by his valet pulling back the curtains.

"Eight o'clock, Your Grace!"

"Eight o'clock?" the Duke repeated. "I must get up. I want to leave here before nine."

"Hanson asked me to tell Your Grace he's collected the Phaeton and there was no trouble about it."

The Duke smiled.

He had instructed Hanson last night that he and his other coachman were to drive over to Mr. Newall's house and pick up the Phaeton at dawn.

He was quite certain by this time after their escape Captain Daltry and his conspirators would not have hung about.

They would have gone back to London realising there was nothing to do but accept their losses and hope he would not take legal action against them.

If he was right in his supposition that they would have cleared out, it would be easy for his own servants to pick up the Phaeton and bring it here for him to use today.

He thought with satisfaction that his first change of horses was only about twenty miles away from Lord Armitage's house.

Therefore the extra journey they had taken at dawn would not overtire his team as they had had a good rest.

Everything was going according to plan, the Duke thought, as he bathed then dressed in the clothes that had been on the brake, and which made him look extremely smart.

His boots had such a shine on them that they seemed to reflect like mirrors.

"Where shall we be meeting Your Grace tonight?" the valet enquired as he helped him into an extremely smart jacket which had only recently been delivered by his tailor.

"I will let you know that after I have discussed it with Lady Georgina," the Duke replied.

There was a little pause, then the valet replied:

"I thought Your Grace was aware that Her Ladyship 'ad left!"

"Left?" the Duke exclaimed, and the word rang out like a pistol-shot.

"Her maid informs me when I were downstairs that Her Ladyship rang her bell at six o'clock this morning, and when she was dressed in a habit she'd borrowed she'd gone to th' stables."

The Duke did not speak and after a moment his valet went on a little nervously:

"The maid thought 'twas strange, Your Grace, but I tells her I were sure 'twas something Her Ladyship 'ad arranged with Your Grace last night."

The Duke's lips tightened.

What his valet had just said had stunned him and he was finding it hard to believe what he was told.

At the same time he was wondering frantically what he could do about it.

"Go and find the lady's-maid," he ordered, "and ask her if Her Ladyship left a message for me, or perhaps a note."

The way he spoke made his valet, after one startled glance, quickly leave the room.

The Duke stared into the mirror not seeing his own face, but Ilitta's.

"How can you do this to me?" he cried out in his heart.

He knew at that moment he loved her so overwhelmingly, so completely, that he would never rest until he had found her again and even if she intended to hide from him, wherever she had gone, he would discover her.

He was sensible enough to know it was going to be very difficult, and it was important that Lord Armitage should not know that anything was amiss.

He seemed to wait a long time before his valet came hurrying back into the room.

"The maid apologises most profusely, Your Grace," he said, "but it wasn't until I asks her if Her Ladyship 'd left any kind of message that she discovered there was a note on th' dressing-table."

Without answering the Duke almost snatched it from him and walked to the window to open an envelope which had Lord Armitage's crest on it.

Ilitta's writing was somehow as he had expected it to be: the letters beautifully formed, the written words having a grace and beauty that was somehow like herself.

131

Feeling as if everything danced in front of his eyes he read:

"*I have taken Your advice and I am going home. You were right – I could not look after Myself in London without Anybody to protect Me.*

I did not know such Strange things could happen in the World outside.

I can only thank You for being so kind, and for all the nice things You said about my Pictures.

I shall go on Painting, although there will be nobody to appreciate Them. Perhaps one day when I have finished a Picture which I think will please You, I will ask you to accept it from Somebody who will always be Grateful for having known You.

Ilitta."

On either side of her signature there was a small drawing.

It was easy to recognised Lord Armitage as an ageing horse who had been very spirited in his prime.

On the other side was the writhing body of a cobra and the face was so exactly like the *Comtesse*'s that the Duke as he looked at it gave a little chuckle.

He read the letter once, then again.

Then he knew that while desperately afraid that he had lost Ilitta the letter gave him a ray of hope he had not expected.

He was too experienced with women not to realise that when she had drawn the *Comtesse* as a cobra, making the snake's body sinuous and seductive, she had been jealous!

Only a very feminine reaction could have made her draw the face so perceptively, showing all the *Comtesse*'s beauty and sophistication, and at the same time revealing her as greedily possessive and dangerous.

It told the Duke what he had longed to know; that when Ilitta had written her note to him and drawn the

Comtesse at the foot of it, she had been thinking of him not as a protective stag but as a man.

The Duke slipped the letter back into the envelope and put it in his inside pocket.

Then his brain, which had never failed him in any emergency, began almost like a machine to go over all that had happened, analyse it, and draw conclusions which would eventually enable him to find Ilitta.

He stood for such a long time at the window that his valet watching him anxiously wondered what was going on and what his Master was contemplating.

Then as if the Duke had made up his mind he said abruptly:

"I am going down to breakfast. Get everything packed and tell Hanson to bring the Phaeton to the front door in half-an-hour."

"Very good, Your Grace! And the brake?"

"The brake is also to be ready to leave and follow behind."

"Very good, Your Grace!"

The Duke walked down the stairs to the Breakfast Room.

As he expected, Lord Armitage was there, but there was no sign of the *Comtesse*.

"Good morning!" Lord Armitage said heartily. "I hear your pretty sister has already left us and borrowed one of my horses!"

"I must apologise if it is any inconvenience," the Duke replied.

"I gather she is staying somewhere in the neighbourhood," Lord Armitage went on, "and has promised the horse will be returned later today."

This was exactly what the Duke wanted to hear, but he did not wish to appear too eager.

Instead he walked to the sideboard where there was a long array of silver dishes.

As was usual in such country houses, the guests helped

133

themselves to breakfast and there were no servants in attendance.

As he returned to the table he remarked casually:

"Is there anybody near here called Calvert who I hear might have some horses for sale?"

Lord Armitage obviously concentrated on the question before he repeated:

"Calvert? Calvert? I certainly seem to know the name."

Then he shook his head.

"No, I cannot think of anybody called Calvert connected with horses, and I think I know everybody in the County who owns anything on four legs which is worth looking at."

"I may have been mistaken," the Duke said. "Perhaps it is the name of some obscure Squire or Yeoman Farmer."

"Nobody on my land, I think," Lord Armitage replied, "although as I have five thousand acres it is not possible to remember everybody."

"You have as much as that!" the Duke remarked.

"I would have more if I could get it," his host replied. "Between ourselves I rather dislike knowing that Buxworth beats me with seven thousand but at least together we top the poll."

He laughed before he added:

"The others do not even get a 'look in', and they resent it!"

"If you are quite certain there is nobody with the name of Calvert on your estate," the Duke, persisted, "then what about Buxworth's?"

"Of course I cannot speak for him," Lord Armitage replied.

Then he gave an exclamation.

"As I said, the name did ring a bell and now I come to think of it, Buxworth's wife was a Calvert. She died a little over a year ago, and I believe he was broken-hearted at her loss."

"You are sure the name was Calvert?" the Duke asked.

"Yes, I am certain of it!" Lord Armitage replied. "She

was a most attractive woman and very charming. I am not surprised Buxworth misses her, but it has made him more obstinate and self-opinionated than ever!"

"He sounds rather overbearing!"

"Oh, he is all right in his own way," Lord Armitage answered, "but he must be a difficult man to live with. Never listens to anybody's ideas except his own."

"Has he any children?"

"A son in the Army. Nice boy and an excellent rider. He has been overseas for the last three years or so."

There was a pause and the Duke asked tentatively:

"No other children?"

"Let me see," the Marquess replied. "I think there is a young daughter. Yes, I remember now I saw her in the distance at her mother's funeral."

The Duke was silent, but he was no longer hungry, and he drank his coffee quickly.

"If you will forgive me," he said, "I must be on my way."

"Of course!" Lord Armitage agreed, "and it has been a very great pleasure having you here."

"I hope to entertain you before long in Gloucestershire," the Duke replied, "and as I have been filled with admiration for your horses, I hope you will appreciate mine."

"There is no doubt about that," Lord Armitage smiled. "All the same, I shall try to beat you in some of the Steeple-Chases this Autumn, and will definitely be waiting to challenge you on the Flat!"

'I shall look forward to it!" the Duke answered.

In a great hurry to be off, he tipped all the servants handsomely, then almost ran down the steps to climb into his Phaeton which was waiting for him.

Hanson jumped up beside him, Lord Armitage waved goodbye, and they set off down the drive, the brake containing the Duke's luggage, his valet and two other grooms following.

135

They had passed through the gates at the end of the drive before Hanson asked:

"Where are we going, Your Grace?"

There was a smile on the Duke's lips, even though the expression in his eyes was still a little anxious, as he answered:

"To call on the Marquess of Buxworth!"

Chapter Seven

The Duke found his way to the Marquess of Buxworth's house, although he realised that, as Lord Armitage had said, it took very much longer to drive there than if he had been able to travel across country on horseback.

As he drove down a long drive bordered by elm trees he saw the house in front of him, a large, somewhat pretentious mansion which he would not have wished to own himself.

He did however appreciate the number of horses he saw in the fields beyond the park. Even at a distance they looked well-bred and the type of which any owner could be proud.

He however was not thinking of the Marquess, but almost praying, although he would have been embarrassed to admit it, that he would find Ilitta.

All the way he was driving along the narrow twisting lanes he was fitting together like a puzzle, separate fragments of information which she had given him while not intending to, and completing, he thought, what seemed to be a reasonable solution to his problem.

"I must find her, I must!" he resolved.

He knew that because for the moment he had lost her his love had increased until it seemed to burn within him like a furnace.

In all his numerous love-affairs he had never felt for any woman what he was feeling now for Ilitta.

It was as if his whole body was crying out for her, and she drew him as if she were a magnet.

He admitted to himself that in the past he had always

thought of love as something set aside from his other activities.

Although he enjoyed the company of women, he was always perfectly content to go travelling on his own.

Otherwise he spent his time at Race-Courses and in Clubs with men, and had not missed feminine companionship except for the eternal reason that every Adam needs his Eve.

Now he knew that what he wanted of Ilitta was that she should be with him not merely that he could make love to her, but to enable him to talk to her since everything she said stimulated his mind.

Although it seemed almost exaggerated to think so, she complemented him as a complete person.

For the first time in his life he understood as he had never done before, exactly what his father and mother had found in the closeness of each other.

While he had believed it was something which happened only once in a million years, he knew now that he too had been fortunate enough to find a woman whom he could enshrine in his heart and worship for ever.

As he drew his horse to a standstill and handed the reins to Hanson there was an anxious expression in his grey eyes as he stepped out of his Phaeton and walked up a short flight of stone steps to the front door.

It was opened before he reached it, and a footman in the Marquess's livery looked at him in surprise.

The Duke felt as if he held his breath and crossed his fingers before he said:

"I wish to speak to Lady Ilitta!"

As he said her name he felt he was like a gambler throwing all he possessed on the turn of a card.

He knew that if he was mistaken and Ilitta was not here, he had no idea where he could go next to look for her.

There was a slight hesitation before the footman said, as if he was slightly taken aback by the request:

"Her Ladyship's in th' Music Room, Sir, I'll fetch her."

"No, do not do that," the Duke said quickly. "Take me to her."

As he spoke his heart was singing and he knew that his instinct had been sound, his calculations correct, and he had found her!

The footman went ahead of him down a somewhat dark passage in which the Duke appreciated the fine furniture and one or two pictures which he would have liked to own himself.

After walking for some way the footman paused at a large mahogany door and turning to look at the Duke asked:

"What name shall I say Sir?"

"I will announce myself," the Duke replied.

The footman raised his eyebrows, but he was too young and inexperienced to argue and stepped to one side as the Duke opened the door and went into the room.

It flashed through his mind that he had not realised that amongst Ilitta's other talents she was a lover of music.

Then at a glance he saw the reason why she was here, which did not concern the closed piano which stood on a small dais.

In front of the windows which had a North light, with her back to him, she was seated at an easel on which there was a large canvas.

The Duke quietly shut the door behind him and realised she was concentrating so intently on what she was doing that she had not heard him come into the room.

There was a thick carpet on the floor and he walked over it softly until he was near enough to see that what Ilitta was painting was a portrait of himself.

She was not caricaturing him as a stag or any other animal, but he could see an undoubted likeness to his eyes, his square forehead, and his straight nose.

He stood looking at her thinking that her golden hair piled high on top of her head was very attractive.

Then as she hesitated over some colour on her palette

the intensity of his gaze, or perhaps the vibration of his love, made her turn her head.

For a moment she just stared at him incredulously.

Then she jumped to her feet saying:

"Why are you . . here? What has happened? How did you . . find me?"

The questions seemed to tumble over themselves as she stared at the Duke as if he was an apparition from another world.

He walked a little closer to her before he replied:

"I have come to ask you to help me, Ilitta."

"To . . help you?" she questioned. "What has happened . . what has . . gone wrong?"

"Something very serious!"

She put the palette down on a chair before she said:

"You . . you do not mean . . you are not in . . danger?"

There was a little tremor in her voice which the Duke did not miss and he replied quietly:

I am in a position where I must have your help, yours only, and I cannot manage without it."

"I cannot think what can have . . happened!" Ilitta said in a frightened voice. "Is Captain Daltry . . threatening you? You do not . . think he might . . hurt you . . as he intended . . to do?"

Now her eyes were very wide and the Duke saw the fear in them.

He also thought she was trembling.

"It is not Captain Daltry who has upset me."

"Then . . who? And how did you . . find me?"

"I will answer all your questions in a moment," the Duke replied, "but first I want your assurance, your solemn word of honour, Ilitta, that you will help me."

She glanced at the door, almost as if she was afraid her father or somebody else might come in, before she said a little hesitatingly:

"It . . might be . . difficult . . and you should not be . . here."

"Nevertheless I am here!" the Duke replied. "So promise me, please promise me, Ilitta, for I cannot save myself without you."

"I . . do not . . understand," she said, "but you know I will do . . anything you . . ask of me."

There was an intensity in the way she spoke which the Duke wanted to hear.

"You swear to that?" he said in a deep voice.

He held out his hand as he spoke and without hesitating Ilitta placed hers in his.

As his fingers closed over hers he felt them quiver and knew it was because he was touching her.

"You swear you will not let me down?"

"I . . swear it!"

Her eyes as she spoke were looking questioningly into his, and he knew she would not refuse what he asked.

"Thank you," he said softly.

Then as he released her hand he said in an altogether different voice:

"Now tell me how you could dare run away in such a ridiculous fashion? How could you do anything so abominable after all we have been through together?"

She looked away from him and the colour rose in her face.

"I . . I had to go!"

"Why?"

"Y.you told me to . . go home."

"But you did not tell me where your home was."

She was still looking away from him and her features, with her small nose, were silhouetted against the sunshine outside.

The Duke thought it was impossible that anybody could be so beautiful.

He felt his love for her surge within him with the force and power of a tidal wave, but he held himself strictly under control and merely asked very quietly:

"Did you want to leave me, Ilitta?"

"No . . but I had to . . unless I went to London, and I was too afraid to do so . . alone."

"I told you I would take you there."

"I . . I could not have allowed you to . . do that."

"Why not? What made you change your mind? You were quite ready to let me do so before we stayed with Lord Armitage."

She did not answer, but he knew she was debating whether or not to tell him the truth, and after a moment he said:

"I think I am right in saying that you changed your mind when you learnt my real name."

"You should have . . told me who you . . were when we . . first met!"

"Why? And you used a name that was not your own, but your mother's."

She glanced for a moment at him in surprise. Then she asked:

"How did you know that?"

"You must be aware that ever since I learnt this morning that you had run away I have been grasping at every clue that might tell me where you had gone. As it happened the Marquess remembered that your mother was a Calvert."

For a moment a faint smile flickered on Ilitta's lips as she said:

"It was stupid of me not to call myself Smith or Brown or something ordinary like that."

"Did you really wish never to see me again?" the Duke enquired.

"I thought as you were only being . . kind to me, I was becoming somewhat of an . . encumbrance."

"That might have been true the first night we met at the Inn," he said, "but I think after what we suffered together at the hands of the 'Fox, the Ferret and the Baboon', and you slept all night in my arms, our relationship became rather different."

He saw the crimson flood which swept over her cheeks

142

and thought it was the most beautiful thing he had ever seen.

He knew too that for the first time she was acutely conscious that when she had slept so trustingly beside him he had been a man, and her feelings for him now were very different from what they had been then.

Unexpectedly, because it was in his mind, the Duke asked:

"What is the scent you use?"

"Scent?"

She was so astonished that she turned her eyes towards his, then found it impossible to look away.

"My . . scent?" she repeated as if it was hard to understand what they were talking about.

"It has tantalised me because I cannot find a name for it."

"It is White Lilac. My mother taught me how to distil it and we used to make it together, but this is the first time I have made it myself."

"It suits you."

He thought as he spoke that he had not been imaginative enough to realise that as she was the personification of purity there could be no flower that would suit her better than the sweetness and Spring-like quality of the White Lilac.

"Your scent has haunted me just as you have," he said, "and I want to know what you intend to do about it!"

He saw a little tremor run through her because of the way he spoke. Then she said quickly:

"You have asked me to help you . . and please . . although I will do so if you are in danger . . I do not want . . Papa to know you are here."

"You father was expecting me, as you know, a few nights ago," the Duke said, "so I cannot believe he will refuse to receive me, even if I have arrived a trifle late!"

"It is . . not that."

The words seemed to be strangled in Ilitta's throat, and

as if she was afraid to be near the Duke she walked away from him to stand against the window looking into the sunlit garden.

"What is worrying you about my being here?"

He moved nearer to her as he spoke and thought she wanted to run away, but was unable to do so.

He waited for an answer to his question and after a long pause Ilitta said:

"I . . do not . . want to . . tell you!"

"Why not?"

"Because . ."

Her voice died away and he knew she was feeling it was impossible to tell him what he wanted to know.

Instead she turned towards him to say pleadingly:

"Please . . go away . . and forget me . . you were so kind . . so very kind . . but I do not . . belong to your world . . and you have women like the *Comtesse* to amuse you . . I am only somebody who . . came into your life in the fog."

"Do you really think that what happened that night at the Inn," the Duke asked in his deep voice, "and the night we were together in the attic, and our escape from either being starved to death or forced to surrender ignominiously, is something either of us can ever forget?"

"You have . . so many other things in . . your life."

"But now I have something which is so important and so vital that it has always been out of reach."

"What is that?"

She asked the question automatically.

There was a pause before the Duke said very softly:

"Love!"

For a moment Ilitta was very still. Then as if she was frightened by what she had heard she said quickly:

"I . . I do not know . . what you are . . saying."

"I think you do," the Duke answered. "Look at me, Ilitta!"

It was an order and, as if it was impossible to resist him, very slowly she turned her face towards his.

Her eyes looked up at him and he saw that while they were apprehensive and a little perplexed, there was something else, something which he believed was what he was seeking.

For a moment they just stared at each other. Then he said:

"I thought with your perception and your instinct for seeing beneath the surface that you would have known by this time that I love you!"

"It . . cannot be . . true!"

Her voice was almost inaudible.

Then as if she saw the answer in his eyes, the expression on her face changed and a radiance that was unlike anything the Duke had ever seen transformed her.

It made her so beautiful that he felt she must be unreal and that such beauty could only be found in the sunshine.

Then slowly, as if they both moved to music, they seemed to melt into each other without conscious thought, drawn by a magnetism that came from their hearts and souls, and was not really human.

"I love you!" the Duke said.

Even to himself his voice sounded strange.

He bent his head and touched Ilitta's lips gently with his own as if she was a flower.

Then as he felt her softness, her sweetness, her innocence, his arms tightened.

His kiss became more insistent, more demanding, and yet at the same time gentle because she was so precious and he was afraid of frightening her.

To Ilitta it was as if the sky opened and she was suddenly transported into a Heaven that she thought she had lost when she had ridden away at dawn from Lord Armitage's house.

She had awoken during the night to think that the Duke had not come to see her as she had asked him to do.

She was sure it was the *Comtesse* who had detained him, a beautiful, sophisticated woman who had made it very clear that she was attracted to him.

Then at that moment, as if it was written in fire in the darkness, Ilitta had realised she loved the Duke.

She loved his face, his eyes, the twist of his lips, his deep voice, the strength of his arms, his heart she had felt beating all night against her own heart.

It was only later that Ilitta realised it was because of her ignorance of men that she had not recognised earlier her love for the Duke. It had been a strange joy to be with him, even while she had been desperately afraid of what Captain Daltry might do.

She knew, thinking back, that when she had looked down at him through the open trap-door and saw the expression of delight on his face because she had returned, her heart had turned a dozen somersaults.

She had wanted to throw herself into his arms and for him to hold her close and safe against him.

It was love, and yet because she had been so childishly foolish she had merely thought how exciting it had been to tell him how she had found the old man and that they could escape form the Baboon and Captain Daltry's threats.

Then in the comfortable, curtained bed she had thought how the Duke had made her lie beside him to keep warm and how happy and secure she had felt in his arms.

Looking back, she realised how miserable she had been ever since her mother had died and her father had not ceased to bully her into doing what he wanted, and to be utterly indifferent to her feelings and her sense of loss and loneliness.

He had ridiculed her paintings, telling her to occupy her time in a more sensible manner, and there had been nobody to talk to in the big house except servants.

Because they were in deep mourning nobody came to call except men who wanted to talk to her father about horses.

She had drifted around the empty rooms missing her mother unbearably and, because she had been still a school-girl until the beginning of the year, receiving no invitations and meeting nobody of her own age.

"How could I have known there were men in the world like the Duke," she asked herself, "and that he would be so different from what I expected? And how could I have been so foolish as to fall in love with him?"

She had seen the *Comtesse* talking to him provocatively invitingly, and looking so exotically alluring as she did so that Ilitta could understand the Duke being fascinated by her.

How could she think of herself except as a tiresome young girl who had forced herself on him, when there were women like that fawning on him and obviously wildly attracted by him?

Ilitta was so innocent that she had no idea exactly what a man and a woman did when they made love.

When she stayed upstairs for dinner because she was afraid one of Lord Armitage's guests might recognise her, she had been tortured by pictures which flashed before her eyes of the *Comtesse* looking at the Duke.

She could see her hands with their long, sharp nails reaching out to touch him, and her red lips obviously inviting his kisses.

That, Ilitta told herself, was the reason why the Duke had not come to say goodnight to her as she had expected.

He had been kissing the *Comtesse*, kissing her and perhaps he had gone to her bedroom instead of coming to hers.

It was then she knew she could not endure the pain in her breast any longer.

Nor could she possibly face the Duke the next morning, knowing he had no wish to be with her, but preferred to be with the *Comtesse*.

"I must go away," she told herself.

That was the moment when she knew that the only

thing she could do would be to return home.

She made her plans carefully, thinking the Duke would be pleased to be rid of her and would never guess that she was in fact the Marquess of Buxworth's daughter.

She had written a letter to him which she had left on her dressing-table and ringing for the maid asked her if she could borrow a riding habit belonging to Lord Armitage's younger daughter whose clothes she had already found fitted her reasonably well.

"You've got a huge choice, M'Lady," the maid had answered. "Miss Maureen's always buying herself new habits because she's so keen on riding."

Ilitta was not listening, and merely hurried into the habit the maid brought her, promised to return it later in the day, and went to the stables.

Lord Armitage's groom showed no surprise at her request to borrow a horse but thought it strange that she should ride alone.

"I have not far to go," Ilitta told him.

Then when she had tipped him he asked no more questions.

Only as she rode away did she feel as if she was leaving behind a part of herself, and knew it was her heart.

Now as the Duke kissed her, she felt as if the sunshine was not only a dazzling light in their eyes, but a light which came from their souls.

Nobody, she thought, could feel such ecstasy and not die of it.

Then as the Duke kissed her and went on kissing her, she wanted to live and to capture the wonder and glory he was giving her, making it hers for ever.

Finally he raised his head to say in a voice that was hoarse and unsteady:

"My darling, my sweet, how could you have run away from me? I thought I had lost you!"

"I . . love you!"

"That is what I wanted you to say, but I was so afraid that

148

I would frighten you if I told you of my love."

"I could . . never be frightened of . . you!"

"And I will make sure that nobody else frightens you ever again," the Duke vowed.

Then he was kissing her until the whole world seemed to swim dizzily around them.

When at last they came back to earth Ilitta said:

"You . . asked me to . . help you."

"I wanted you to find for me somebody who is so precious, so incredibly wonderful, that I know I cannot live without her."

"You said you were . . desperate!"

"I was desperate when you disappeared. It would have driven me mad if you had not been here as I prayed you might be."

"I never thought for . . one instant that you would . . find me!"

"But I have found you, and I will never lose you again!"

He smiled as he said more lightly:

"Never again, my darling one, will you do anything so outrageous as to travel about the countryside alone."

Ilitta made a little murmur and hid her face against his shoulder.

"How could you take such risks with yourself?"

"I . . I had to get . . away!"

"But, why? I do not understand!"

Ilitta trembled and although it excited him, at the same time he was puzzled.

"Why did you run away?" he asked.

Ilitta's voice was very low as she whispered:

"P.Papa told me . . that the . . Duke of Marazion was coming to . . s.stay!"

"And that upset you? But why?"

"Papa said he was . . sure it was not because you were interested in his stables . . having so many horses yourself . . but because you . . intended to . . m.marry me!"

The words were almost incoherent, and for a moment

149

the Duke stared down at Ilitta as though he could not believe what he had heard.

Then he laughed and it was a sound of genuine amusement before he said:

"That is the last thing that would have entered my mind! But, my darling, what has happened proves that your father was being prophetic, for I have every intention of marrying his daughter!"

He paused, then added:

"If, of course, she will have me!"

She looked up into his eyes, then drew in her breath.

"I . . love you," she said, "but I never thought of being . married to the . . Duke of Marazion!"

"When did you first know you loved me?"

"I . . I did not realise it until yesterday . . when you became the . . Duke . . then there was the . . *Comtesse*."

". . Whom you saw as a cobra," the Duke finished, "and you were quite right, my darling. That is exactly what she is, and I have an aversion to snakes. I very skilfully prevented myself from being involved with her."

"Is . . that true?"

"I promise you it is. When I came up to bed I came to your bedroom to say goodnight to you, but you were asleep."

"You . . came? You really . . came?"

"I came!" the Duke repeated, "and because I was thinking of you, my precious little love, I merely kissed your hair and went away."

Ilitta's eyes shone like stars as she said:

"I never imagined that you had done that!"

"I went to bed," the Duke said, "and lay thinking about you until I fell asleep."

"I wish I had . . known."

"I cannot think what has happened to your intuition if you were not aware what I was feeling for you, and how much I wished I had not brought you to Lord Armitage's house."

150

"It was very stupid of me to let you do so," Ilitta answered, "but after we got free all I could think of was that I wanted to be with you and escape from those horrible men."

"I was thinking the same thing," the Duke admitted, "and that is why I did not tell you my real name."

"I never dreamt . . I never imagined for one instant that you could be the Duke from whom I had . . run away!"

"And I never dreamt that was the reason why you had left home!" the Duke laughed.

"I had always sworn to myself that I would never ever marry any man unless I loved him," Ilitta said, "and I had the terrifying feeling that any husband Papa chose for me, as he was determined to do, would look like some unpleasant animal, and I would therefore hate him!"

"I wonder whether, if you had met me in the ordinary way, I should have appeared to you as a Royal," the Duke pondered, "or, as you say, something very unpleasant."

"You are no longer an . . animal," Ilitta said quickly, "but a god who has come down from Olympus and I cannot believe it is possible that you . . love me."

"I will make you sure of that," the Duke replied, "and, darling, I intend to marry you immediately! But first you must meet my mother. She has been praying for years that I should find a perfect wife and will be very thrilled that her prayers have been answered."

"I would love to meet her," Ilitta said, "and I think you are very lucky that your mother is still alive."

"I know I am," the Duke agreed. "Now let us make plans, my precious one. First, how we can go away together tomorrow morning without your father thinking it a very strange thing for us to do."

Ilitta thought it over. Then she said:

"Are you suggesting . . really intending that we need not tell . . Papa what we feel about each other?"

"My instinct," the Duke replied, "makes me feel sure that it will upset you, or at least be something that will embarrass you, if your father thinks that he is negotiating our marriage and takes all the credit for it."

"That is clever of you! It would somehow . . spoil what we feel for each other, and my marriage would seem exactly as if he were selling one of his horses to the highest bidder."

The Duke laughed.

"I am certainly prepared to pay anything he asks," he said, "but I know exactly what you are saying, my dearest heart, and so I have an idea!"

Ilitta put her cheek against his shoulder.

"I love you, and because I love you I am so happy that I am quite certain I am dreaming."

"I am sure I am too," the Duke said. "But this is true, my darling–I have never in my life felt about any woman as I feel about you."

"How . . do you feel?"

"Very excited and so elated that I have found you that I feel as if I am jumping over every fence of the Grand National Course with a foot to spare!"

Ilitta laughed and he thought it was the prettiest sound he had ever heard.

"I feel the same!" she said quickly. "Quickly! Tell me your plan before Papa comes back from the gallops."

"Is that where he has gone?"

"Of course! That is where he always goes in the morning. He is quite certain he has two horses that will beat yours next time they run!"

"He can beat any horse I have in my stable," the Duke said, "as long as I can marry you."

"You can do that now today – or tomorrow!"

"It is what I want too, my precious one, but I think it would cause a scandal and not only shock your father, but upset my mother."

"Then what can we do?" Ilitta asked.

"What I am going to suggest," the Duke said, "is that when your father returns I will tell him that despite the

152

letter of apology he received this morning, I thought it might appear that I had been rude, unless I came in person to explain how the fog prevented me from reaching him."

"He will be so delighted to see you that he will not worry about anything else."

"That should make it easier," the Duke said. "Then I want you to tell him in my presence that you have had a letter asking you to stay with a friend in Gloucestershire."

He smiled before he went on:

"I shall tell your father that by amazing coincidence I am travelling to Gloucestershire myself, and if he will allow me, I will be delighted to escort you there early tomorrow morning. Your lady's maid can travel in my brake behind us."

Ilitta clapped her hands.

"You are so clever! I might have known you would think of a perfectly reasonable explanation for my travelling with you, Besides, as Papa wishes me to get married, he will think it an excellent way of our getting to know each other better."

"Which is exactly what I want myself," the Duke said. "Not only to know you better, my lovely one, but to make sure that you are mine, now and forever, and that there is no chance of your ever running away from me again!"

"You need not be afraid of that," Ilitta said. "How could I ever want to . . leave you when I love you . . and there is nobody in the world but . . you?"

There was a touch of passion in her voice that the Duke had not heard before, and it made him pull her almost roughly against him to kiss her demandingly, fiercely, as if he was making sure she was his and she could never escape him.

Ilitta was not afraid, she only felt as if she was being carried on wings to Olympus, and if he was a god he had made her his goddess.

Their feelings were too ecstatic, too perfect to be anything but Divine.

Only when the intensity of what they were feeling made them both breathless did Ilitta with a little murmur hide her face against him again.

"God, how I love you!" the Duke exclaimed. "How could I have ever guessed that love could be so different from any emotion I have ever known or felt before?"

"It is . . wonderful . . perfect . . but you must teach me how to make you . . happy, so that you will never be . . disappointed."

"I could never be that."

He kissed her hair as he spoke and thought the scent of White Lilac was a magic spell which held him captive for ever.

Then with a hint of laughter in his voice he said:

"Despite all I have heard about your instinct, you ran away from me, although fate meant you to marry the Duke of Marazion."

"I cannot imagine why I was so stupid," Ilitta said. "But actually it was a fog which brought us together."

"Or rather, a gentleman to whom I shall always be grateful for sending you scurrying into my bedroom for safety."

"How can you say such things?" Ilitta asked, but she was laughing and her eyes were shining.

"You will certainly have to start writing the book that we have planned for our children and our grandchildren."

He watched the flush creeping up her face and added:

"You must illustrate it, and although they will have to be kept under lock and key, I am looking forward to the drawings you will do for me of my friends, my enemies and everybody important you will meet as the Duchess of Marazion."

Ilitta gave a little choked laugh. Then she said:

"I expected you would tell me I was never to draw again."

"I shall insist upon your drawing," the Duke said, "but will constitute myself as censor of what may be shown to other people, and what is especially for me."

"They will all be for *you*," Ilitta cried, "just as everything I do and everything I think will be for you exclusively!"

The Duke knew this was exactly what he had always wanted his wife to feel.

Because there were no words to express the happiness which was running through him he pulled Ilitta back into his arms and found her lips.

As he kissed her he knew he was setting out on an adventure that was so thrilling, so exciting that nothing he had ever done in his life before would equal it.

Once again he was the winner, the victor, the conqueror, only this time he had gained the ultimate reward of all—a love that could only have come from Heaven.

Other books by Barbara Cartland

Romantic Novels, over 370, the most recently published being:

Light from the Gods
From Hate to Love
Love on the Wind
The Duke Comes Home
Journey to a Star
Love and Lucia
The Unwanted Wedding
Gypsy Magic
Help from the Heart
A Duke in Danger

Lights, Laughter and a Lady
The Unbreakable Spell
Diona and a Dalmatian
Fire in the Blood
The Scots Never Forget
The Rebel Princess
A Witch's Spell
Secrets
The Storms of Love
Moonlight on the Sphinx

The Dream and the Glory
(in aid of the St John Ambulance Brigade)

Autobiographical and Biographical
The Isthmus Years 1919-1939
The Years of Opportunity 1939-1945
I Search for Rainbows 1945-1976
We Danced All Night 1919-1929
Ronald Cartland (with a Foreword by Sir Winston Churchill)
Polly My Wonderful Mother
I Seek the Miraculous

Historical
Bewitching Women
The Outrageous Queen (The story of Queen Christina of Sweden)
The Scandalous Life of King Carol
The Private Life of Elizabeth, Empress of Austria
Josephine, Empress of France
Diane de Poitiers
Metternich — the Passionate Diplomat
The Private Life of Charles II

Sociology

You in the Home	Etiquette
The Fascinating Forties	The Many Facets of Love
Marriage for Moderns	Sex and the Teenager
Be Vivid, Be Vital	The Book of Charm
Love, Life and Sex	Living Together
Vitamins for Vitality	The Youth Secret
Husbands and Wives	The Magic of Honey
Men are Wonderful	Book of Beauty and Health

Keep Young and Beautiful by Barbara Cartland and Elinor Glynn

Cookery
Barbara Cartland's Health Food Cookery Book
Food for Love
Magic of Honey Cookbook
Recipes for Lovers

Editor of
The Common Problems by Ronald Cartland (with a preface by the Rt. Hon. the Earl of Selborne,PC)
Barbara Cartland's Library of Love
Barbara Cartland's Library of Ancient Wisdom
"Written with Love" Passionate love letters selected by Barbara Cartland

Drama
Blood Money
French Dressing

Philosophy
Touch the Stars

Radio Operetta
The Rose and the Violet (music by Mark Lubbock) performed in 1942

Radio Plays
The Caged Bird: An episode in the Life of Elizabeth Empress of Austria. Performed in 1957

General
Barbara Cartland's Book of Useless Information, with a
Foreword by The Earl Mountbatten of Burma (in aid of the
United Colleges)
Love and Lovers (Picture Book)
The Light of Love (Prayer Book)
Barbara Cartland's Scrapbook (in Aid of the Royal
Photographic Museum)
Romantic Royal Marriages
Barbara Cartland's Book of Celebrities

Verse
Lines on Life and Love

Music
An Album of Love Songs sung with the Royal Philharmonic
Orchestra

Film
The Flame is Love

Cartoons
Barbara Cartland's Romances (book of cartoons) has
recently been published in the U.S.A and Great Britain and in
other parts of the world